ERIC P. JOHNSON

Called of Kristoff

A Santa Chronicle

Third edition

ISBN: 9798998759420

This book was professionally typeset on Reedsy.
Find out more at reedsy.com

Contents

1

The Persuasion on Piccadilly Street

Joseph Amesbury dug his fingernails deep into the wooden armrests of the chair, his heart galloping wildly from the release of adrenaline. Luckily for the reporter, an ear-popping crack from an ember smoldering in the ashy fireplace brought back the distracted man's attention to the conversation.

"Can you hear me properly, lad?" the wrinkled elderly man respectfully questioned his visitor across the dimly lit room. "I dare say you can understand me properly, can't you?"

Joseph was a tall man in his late thirties and today dressed in a neatly pressed blue suit that accentuated his broad shoulders and complimented his muscular build. Guilty and embarrassed by being called out, an earlier statement from the portly fellow had caused Joseph's mind to drift.

"A million pardons, sir." The apology, heavily drenched in a British accent, fumbled out of his mouth. Joseph scrambled for the right words to cover up his wandering mind. "I do apologize. You see, sir, it's not your grasp of the English language that I'm struggling with. No, not in the slightest. It's that...I—" Joseph wrinkled his nose. "It's that I,

1

uh…I detect from your accent that you are of Germanic origin. Am I correct?" Joseph had always been quick-fire under pressure. Being a sharp-witted reporter, Joseph used a delay tactic to buy him additional time and come up with a question to hide his wandering mind.

Reaching up, Joseph peeled off his felt hat, exposing thick black hair that was plastered backward from the use of his favorite mocha fedora. His sapphire blue eyes were kind and inviting, though his personal grooming today hadn't included a razor, evident by the dark

stubble protruding out of his sharp jawline. After a brief silent pause, Joseph once again felt confident and firmly collected in his thoughts. "May I inquire as to your former place of residence? Dare I say…Berlin?" Joseph angrily thought, *How could I be in this room with this dodgy lunatic? This old man is as mad as a bag of ferrets. After all, how could any sane person make such a preposterous claim? Claiming to know how to do magic tricks is one thing, but to declare yourself to be a magical creature of folklore is over-the-top barmy—completely insane.*

Joseph's thoughts were interrupted by the soft, reverent voice of the white-bearded man sitting across from him.

"Berlin, you suspect, eh? Now that brings back many memories." The old man's voice cracked as he continued, "Both painful and good memories. You see, dear lad, Berlin is where the story begins for me. Over eighty years ago, the searing pain of war was etched deep into my soul. The genesis of an eternal friendship was formed. Most importantly, this is where I discovered that there are divinely chosen people who have been placed in a very dark world in order to help soften the ever-hardening human heart. These wonderful individuals help retain peace and hope." The elderly man's words trailed off as he stared blankly at the flames licking the smoldering logs. Joseph sighed and sat back in the chair digesting the tender words of the old man.

––––––––––––––

The start of the day's events in downtown London commenced with Joseph feverishly trying to beat his article deadline. He had just handed his news article to the editor when a button-nosed, middle-aged woman with soft, rounded arch eyebrows and emerald green eyes burst into the room. "Mr. Amesbury!" the half-winded woman blurted out. "Yes, Ms. Dixson?" Joseph replied sharply, feeling frustrated by her intrusion. "What can I help you with?" His deep blue eyes zeroed in on the woman. "Well, get on with it. I don't have all day," he grumbled.

"Why, sir, the *Gazette* received an intriguing call from an elderly man requesting a private interview with the most seasoned reporter of our agency." Her voice was now subdued. "Mr. Amesbury, the man called you out by name and insisted that the interview occur tonight at eight o'clock in his home. The caller stated that he wished to reveal one of the world's greatest secrets in his final days of life. Once disclosed to you, it would be life-altering."

Ms. Dixson's remarks abruptly changed Joseph's demeanor. He reached back, grabbed the edge of a well-worn desk chair, and pulled it slowly toward himself. He perched himself on the edge of his chair and ignoring his dusty, unused computer, snatched a stubby pencil and jotted down his racing thoughts. *Life-altering secret to be shared. What kind of secret? How will it alter or change my life?*

"Excuse me, Ms. Dixson. Did the caller leave any additional details?" asked Joseph in a more hushed tone.

"Only directions to get to his flat, sir. Not a home address, only directions, or rather, a description of how to arrive at his home."

"Very well. Just leave the directions there on the entry table, and that will be all for today."

"Should I just text you the address?" she said in a snarky voice, knowing he did not own a cell phone. Joseph rolled his eyes, dismissing her suggestion.

Ms. Dixson did as requested and turned to head out of the office.

"Wait!" Joseph called out to his secretary.

"Yes, sir?" she responded.

"Thank you, Annabel. I know it is not easy at times to work for me when I am under a deadline. I can be a bit gobby," he said tenderly. This was the first time Joseph had addressed his assistant by her first name.

Ms. Dixson's face flashed a tell-tale shade of red and turning sharply on her polished black shoes, she headed for the door. With her back to Mr. Amesbury, a smile sheepishly stretched across her heart-shaped face. "See you in the morning, Joseph." Grinning from ear to ear, she sashayed out the door. Joseph reached up and grasped the knot of his necktie. Pulling downward, he loosened the snuggly fit neckwear and then popped open the top button of his shirt. With enamored eyes, the reporter stared at his secretary until she disappeared out of sight.

Composing himself, Joseph felt himself begin to melt into his chair, and for the next three hours, he did not budge from his seat. Determined to catch up with his work once and for all, he chipped away at the neglected tower of uncompleted work piled up on his desk. Multiple stapled papers of varying thickness towered over the edge of the plastic inbox, spilling onto the floor. Glancing downward, Joseph eyed a tan certificate with an elegant green rosette vintage woodcut border and a faux gold seal in the center. In classic Baskerville font, Joseph was honored once again for his excellence in journalism.

Over the years, Joseph Amesbury had become a well-known name among reporters, the press, and the journalism world. Perhaps his traditional methods of investigative work and his stubborn refusal to use electronic devices are some of the reasons why he became such a good reporter; he had to work harder to get to the facts. Bending over, Joseph snatched the certificate and heaved open his lower right desk drawer. The heavy drawer was filled to capacity with numerous certificates, journalism awards, and even two George Cross medals for saving multiple lives. On two separate occasions, while investigating journalism assignments, he was, as some say, at the wrong place at the wrong time. However, for those whose life was in peril, Mr. Amesbury was in the right place at the right time. Between both disasters combined, he had saved over forty people from certain doom. James was never one to boast or seek personal recognition for those rescues. In his mind, any accolades from those experiences were best kept in a drawer or out of sight. In humility, he would always tell others that he was only doing what any person would have done in the same circumstances.

Intensely involved with his work that day, Joseph failed to realize that several hours had slipped away since his secretary had departed for the evening. Gazing upward at the clock on the wall, the numbers all melted together. *Is that hand pointing at a six or a seven?* He wondered. Within a few moments and several additional attempts of rubbing the blur out of his eyes, it became clear, that the small hand was pointing directly at the number seven.

Joseph sat stroking his chin, his eyes fixed on the wadded-up pieces of paper scattered across the desk. Consumed by his work, he had been entirely unaware that he was the only employee remaining in the office.

Dang, I did it again, he thought as he ran his fingers through his thick hair. "I worked right through the dinner hour," he moaned as if someone was listening. Scooping up his partially completed pile of work, he crammed it deep inside his tattered buffalo leather briefcase and bolted for the door.

It wasn't until he reached for his fedora hat that he noticed a note paperclipped to the well-worn brim. "8:00 sharp!" was penned by his secretary in jumbo writing and followed by rather peculiar directions. "Turn down the street to your right and walk until you see a white miniature schnauzer crossing your path. Then follow the street on your left until you reach the small gelato shop with the frosted front windows. Go inside the parlor and ask for the salted caramel. (It's one of my personal favorites.) Await further instructions."

Joseph chuckled in disbelief at the note, folded it in half, and tucked it into his coat pocket. Securing his hat, he walked out the front door, forgetting his briefcase of completed work behind.

As he stepped away from his office into the busy city street, his fatigue was exchanged with a burst of new energy. Curiosity had now replaced the need for well-deserved sleep. Grabbing the note out of his pocket, Joseph reread the memo. However, this time, the hurried reporter noticed a significant problem: the memo failed to provide a starting point for the directions.

"This is pure rubbish! What good are directions if you don't know where the bloody starting point is?" he sputtered loudly as if giving a serious ear-bashing to his secretary, who had scribbled the note. Feeling frustrated, he crumpled the paper, shoved it deep into the inside pocket of his heavy trench coat, and stepped off the sidewalk onto the intersection's crosswalk, unaware it was not safe to cross yet. From the corner of his eye, an approaching red double-decker city tour bus filled his vision, and before he knew it, he was laying nose down on the street.

His eyelids clenched as Joseph lay on the cold, black pavement, unsure if he had been pushed from behind or possibly struck by the passing bus. He listened intently to the surrounding street noises and mentally inspected his body for pain or trauma. Voices of concerned pedestrians and the bus puttering away filled his ear canals.

"Gosh, I thought he was a goner," exclaimed a slender fellow on the sidewalk.

"Me too," another voice chimed in.

Opening his eyes, Joseph rolled over and was greeted by an elderly man's chubby hand extending down to hoist him up. Gripping the good Samaritan's hand, Joseph jumped to his feet, dusting the street dirt off his clothes.

"You alright, sir?" a middle-aged woman holding a bag of groceries asked.

"The only thing that hurts is my pride," Joseph said with warm red cheeks.

"Could have been much worse, you know. You are very fortunate," the woman replied.

The reporter straightened his back and, heeding the signal to walk, followed the crowd of onlookers across the crosswalk and down the street, passing by multiple stores, bars, and cafés. He hadn't walked very far before he felt peckish and the grumble from his stomach was a painful reminder that dinner had been neglected, and his gut was demanding his immediate attention. He continued zig-zagging west down a busy sidewalk full of people dashing about and bumping into one another. A hurried woman with her eyes locked on her phone collided with him splashing the remainder of her latte all over the front of his coat. The woman glared at him as if it was his fault that he was walking down her private sidewalk. As quickly as the woman had smashed into him, she was gone, focusing once again on her phone. *Just look up once in a while. Your missing life all around you*, he thought.

Various aromas of prepared foods wafted through the air and floated just above his head. At times, it was tempting to walk on his tippy toes just so he could better indulge in the heavenly scent. Suddenly, his nose caught hold of a distinctive smell. It was the familiar odor of an unforgettable meal his mother had made innumerable times for him as a kid, good old bangers and mash. This childhood delicacy became one of Joseph's favorite meals over the years, and the thought of partaking in the savory sausages and potatoes proved to be just too much for him to resist. He quickly abandoned his previous quest to interview the old man and embarked on a new crusade. Like a bloodhound with its tenacious tracking instinct, Joseph pressed forward on his pursual to discover the creator behind the tempting odor.

Continuing on his way and passing by several storefronts, the hungry man soon found himself rooted outside of a small, busy pub and peered in through the front window of the establishment. The smell of sausages permeated through the open-framed glass door, luring him inside like a bear to honey. Peering through the doorway and past the happy diners, he scanned the room, and his eyes zeroed in on an A-framed blackboard sign leaning against the wall with the following inscription, "Yesterday's special: Bangers and Mash. Thursday's special: Bangers and Mash. Tomorrow's special: Mash and Bangers." It was apparent to Joseph that his well-tuned sniffer didn't steer him wrong. This was indeed the place to satiate his dietary deficiency. Staggered in the front walkway of this gray brick building were four small round tables just big enough for two people. Curiously, all seats outside were vacant, which allowed the reporter to take a short rest while waiting for his order to be taken.

Pulling the dry wicker chair away from the table closest to the front door, he collapsed into the padded seat. His stomach let out another spontaneous grumble.

Settle down in there, He thought while poking his stomach as if trying to pacify it.

At length, a wispy-haired brunette with narrow shoulders and a flashy smile came to his table. "Welcome to the pub. What can I get you?"

The young woman's gentle, inquisitive voice and light pink-colored lips were enough to momentarily cause him to forget his hunger, along with the reason he was sitting at this pub.

"Oh, uh…yes," he clumsily muttered. "I will take yesterday's special please."

"Will that be all?" the young woman pressed.

"Yes," he responded, "that will do."

"Very well," the waitress acknowledged and abruptly turned to walk away.

"Wait a moment," exclaimed Joseph. "Make that… tomorrow's special instead."

The woman gave a courtesy chuckle to his request and, while turning to walk away, rolled her big blue eyes. It was obvious this was not the first time she had heard this cheesy line.

Joseph settled deep into his chair like an old cowboy sitting on a well-worn saddle. The well-deserved rest he received while sitting in the chair was enough to momentarily relieve his feet from pain inflicted by the rapid pursuit of food in his new brown dress shoes. He sat alone in his thoughts watching the hectic pedestrians dashing around to their various destinations. His eyes darted back and forth examining the people passing by the pub in both directions. The motion of moving bodies and the hypnotic rhythm of his eyes helped him relax. Slowly, he slipped deeper and deeper into his thoughts, reflecting back on his childhood. Gradually the sound of the hurried feet pressing down on the sidewalk and the distant muffled voices became less of a distraction to Mr. Amesbury, who had completely zoned out.

Joseph had been adopted at the tender age of three by a loving late middle-aged couple who were unable to have children of their own. Upon being adopted, he instantly became this couple's center of attention and enjoyed his childhood years in a loving environment where he had been taught the difference between right and wrong and the value of hard work. Friday nights were his favorite evening of the week. His mother had established bangers and mash as the evening meal that night. Joseph would run to the table and would often show up ten minutes early.

Joseph's adoptive father worked as an accountant and often got home on Fridays just as the steaming bangers were being placed on the warm bed of potatoes. It was always a delightful evening with his parents, and he cherished them dearly. Unfortunately, his time with his adoptive parents ended early. When Joseph was twenty-two, his parents were involved in a fatal car accident while he was away on one of his first reporting assignments, leaving the young reporter orphaned once again. Joseph never knew his biological parents, and no record of them existed. As a baby, Joseph had been wrapped in a bundle of blankets and abandoned on the steps of an old church when he was only a few days old.

His brief period of semiconsciousness was interrupted by something below the table tugging on his shoestring. Startled by the movement around his feet, Joseph cautiously peeked beneath the table. To his astonishment, a snow-white dog the size of a bowling ball with pointed ears, dark eyes, and a bushy beard had somehow wandered here undetected and taken up residence next to his feet. The stray appeared annoyed that it was sharing a small space with a pair of human legs and attempted to pull Joseph's feet out from under the table. The reporter gently tapped his foot against the soft shoulder of the pooch, hoping to shoo it away. Luckily, the foot nudge was just enough force to send the startled dog on his way.

The reporter watched as the well-groomed, white, stubby-tailed dog trotted away from the pub and down the now unusually quiet street. The retreating dog abruptly stopped in the middle of the road, craned its head back toward the table, and locked eyes with his evictor. The little tyke tilted his left ear to the ground and then, in a forward sweeping motion of his head, gestured to the reporter to follow him. The dog repeated this motion several more times, and Joseph couldn't help but feel that somehow the dog was trying to persuade him to pursue it. Testing his impression to follow the pooch, he sat forward in his chair, giving the impression he was going to stand up. As expected, the dog responded by heading back down the street. Realizing the man was not in pursuit, the dog stopped, turned its head back, and once again made eye contact. It was at that moment that Joseph confirmed that the little schnauzer definitely wanted Joseph to follow him.

2

Schlitten

Intrigued by the white schnauzer's peculiar behavior, Joseph leapt to his feet and thrust his right hand deep into his left inside coat pocket. Palpating the crinkled paper in his fingertips, he yanked the note from his pocket and smoothed it out on the small wooden pub table in front of him. The shock of what he re-read struck with such force that his pulse surged and stomach lurched. He read, "Turn down the street to your right when a small white miniature schnauzer crosses your path…"

Could this be possible? he thought.

Jumping up from the pub table and rushing after the dog, he blurted out, "Well, only one way to find out."

Joseph trailed the schnauzer several yards down the street, away from Piccadilly and the crowd of people strolling by. He soon found himself secluded on an unusually narrow cobblestone street that had been abused by a history of carriages and years of modern-day motored vehicles. The cracked sidewalks were eerily void of pedestrians this evening, and scattered streetlights dotting the street had been intermittently darkened, leaving patches of blackness on either side of him. Pausing to take a look back at the pub where he had just departed, he sighted the zippy brunette waitress heading to his now vacant table carrying a hubcap-sized plate with vapors of stream rising upward. His stomach let out another grumble of protest, and for a brief moment, he was tempted to head back for dinner. At that very moment, a thought popped into his mind. *What if the schnauzer he had been chasing was actually the starting point of the directions scribbled on the small, wrinkled paper?* Once again, he would need to abandon his dinner if he had any hope of making sense of this unusual quest.

Joseph turned his back to the pub and set off to discover, once and for all, who the desperate bloke was behind this elaborate scheme to get a news article interview.

This must be one desperate individual for him to go through such measures just to get an interview with him, he thought. Despite his frustrations of following such silly directions, the intrigue was sufficient enough to spur him forward, though it felt ridiculous to such an accomplished reporter.

Strolling down the silent, ill-lighted street, the tenacious man's mind began to wonder, and he soon found himself in serious personal reflection.

Mr. Amesbury was a kind gentleman who demonstrated selfless acts of kindness throughout his life. He always felt as if he were born with this trait; however, on the opposite spectrum, he was also known to be what some in the office referred to as a workaholic and selfishly guarded his time away from social pleasures so he could meet deadlines. His professional life had consumed him to the point of taking over some of his most notable and compassionate attributes. He felt like he was in a bit of a tug-of-war with his career and his ability to do what he truly loved most, caring for people and providing service to those in need. His passion for success and reaching personal goals had suppressed the innermost true desires of his heart.

At length, his self-inspection abated, and he soon realized that he had meandered quite further down the street searching for the gelato shop. The dirty brick buildings on either side of him appeared to be more run down, damaged, and on the verge of being condemned. Piles of fractured bricks, rubble, and twisted debris were scattered throughout the street. The air was thick, heavy, and difficult to breathe. The scene echoed that of a distant WWII air raid bombing. No lights from windows could be seen, and all streetlights were darkened, snuffing out any shadows. Destruction was everywhere, the street completely abandoned of life. Joseph slid his moist palms into his jacket pocket and continued shuffling along the vacant street. He felt utterly uneasy and vulnerable in these odd new surroundings. *Something strange is going on here*, he thought. *I don't recall this neighborhood.*

A warm illumination down the street could be seen flickering in the distance about half a block away and appeared to be beckoning him. This was the first inviting light he had seen in quite some time. Puzzlingly, something about the flickering light gleaming from the dark comforted him. Hoping to encounter someone inside, he picked up his pace towards the possible safe haven. With every step, Joseph was better able to make out the details of the freshly painted red dwelling poised in front of his gaze. The brick structure had a small green overhanging roof well-positioned to keep patrons dry on rainy days or cast a comforting shadow at high noon. Dangling from the underside of the roof was a lit sign swaying back and forth in the gentle night's breeze. The squeaky flickering sign grabbed the attention of approaching patrons and its malfunctioning electrical system served as a great crowd puller.

Twenty paces away from the store, Joseph paused momentarily to better take in his surroundings from a safe distance. He did not sense any danger around him; however, he was slightly perplexed regarding the neighborhood. It was disheveled, but curiously, here stood a perfectly kept store, which indeed appeared to be well-frequented. Drawing in close to the red brick building, he noted the enormous, frosted glass window panes that covered the entire storefront reflected evidence of being touched by an artistic hand. Scenes of snow-covered hills and majestic pine trees had been carefully etched into the glass with such detail, that it gave a frosty look of reality. Dime-sized snowflakes had also been carefully scratched into the glass, magically refracting light from inside the store, giving it the appearance that the flakes were floating carelessly to the ground.

A suspended, weathered, wooden sign dangled overhead and portrayed the detailed craftsmanship of a skilled carpenter with a fine eye for detail. Though the natural wood aged over the years, it was easy to read the intricately carved border and raised lettering painted in red: **Schlitten Gelato Shop**.

The chiseled board had been fastened to a set of reindeer antlers hanging from two brass chains attached to the undersurface of the porch awning. Small, warm-white incandescent Christmas lights adorned the entire ensemble, creating an inviting glimmer and a sense of comfort to all that gazed upon it. The soft evening breeze tickled the hair on the back of Joseph's head and gently pushed the wooden sign, swinging it back and forth while its lights twinkled in the smooth, rhythmic movement. Joseph concluded that this was the same mesmerizing light that caught his attention half a block away.

From the corner of his eye, a human-shaped shadow inside the store caught his focus. Startled by the movement, he whipped his head to the left to catch a better view. The dark figure appeared to be pacing the wooden floor like a caged animal in the zoo, anxious for his next meal. The reporter cautiously pressed his moist forehead against the chilled glass to get a better view of the person inside. The instant his warm skin rubbed against the cold glass, the shadow figure came to a dead stop, abruptly turned, and raced toward the front door where Joseph was sneaking a peek.

3

A Solemn Declaration

Startled by the approaching individual, Joseph instinctively jumped backward to protect himself. In a split second, the front door flew open, revealing a thin elderly chap donning knee-length green lederhosen with elaborate gold thread embroidery work stitched on the front and lining the pockets. His suspenders were strapped over the top of a neatly pressed white long-sleeved shirt that was rolled up just below the elbow crease, and tall, tight white socks emphasized that his chicken legs curved outward at the knees.

"Good evening, sir. Welcome to the Schlitten Gelato Shop!" a scratchy, high-pitched voice called out. "My name is Eckerd, and I am here to serve you this evening." He straightened up like a maître d' in a fancy restaurant.

Joseph was taken aback by the abrupt presentation and this man's unusual wardrobe selection, and he let out a deep chuckle. He scanned Eckerd up and down, noting the dirty, round-framed spectacles perched on the bridge of the man's large, hooked nose. Eckerd's long sparse white beard was waving in the cool outdoor breeze and covered the wrinkles on his face. His crooked teeth were enveloped in a contagious smile.

"Wow!" said Joseph. "You sure know how to welcome a patron."

Eckerd's smile grew even wider, accentuating the deep lines in the corners of his eyes. "Our policy at the gelato shop is to make everyone that enters those doors feel special, almost celebrity-like."

"Well, I sure felt something, that's for sure!"

The bowlegged man invited his only customer of the night into the store and out of the breezy walkway. A shoulder-height, glass-case freezer filled with cartons of gelato ran the entire length of the wall to his left and along the back wall, forming an L shape. The wall directly to his right was filled with knick-knacks, souvenirs, Christmas ornaments, and screen-printed shirts advertising the gelato shop. Various sized wooden-framed black-and-white photographs were displayed on the interior walls of the building. Each framed photograph was of a horse-drawn sleigh, and every model of the sleigh was different and unique from the others. A large menu board displaying gelato flavors was hanging on the left wall near the 1920's era bronze cash register. Eight small tables filled the remainder of the room, each with four tiny chairs crowded next to them.

Joseph stood in the middle of the gelato shop, trying to wrap his head around all that had transpired that evening. Moments before walking into the shop, he had walked through a sort of war-riddled vacant street only to be greeted by a man fit to work at the local carnival.

"Pardon me, sir, but may I bother you with a question regarding this neighborhood?" he asked.

"Why certainly," the man replied. "Anything for our special guest."

"Splendid. I would like to inquire regarding the rubble in the streets and the condition of this neighborhood. You see, it looked like a scene from a WWII photograph after a bombing run," the reporter explained.

"Oh, you did see that, did you?"

"See it?" Joseph responded incredulously, "Oh, I more than saw it. In fact, I had to walk over most of it. So what gives?"

"All questions in life will eventually discover their paired answer, kind sir. Be it known to you this night that you walked through a history lock."

"I'm sorry, did you say a history lock? Sorry if I appear ignorant, but I am not quite following you."

"Well, I don't expect you to understand quite yet. You just barely arrived at the shop. A history lock is an event in life associated with deep emotion that becomes locked in time. Most people cannot see them, nor do they know they exist. At times, sadness, fear, or exceedingly blissful emotions can re-create the event. They do not last very long. Go see for yourself."

Joseph walked back to the frosted front window and peered out. The street was no longer empty or littered with destruction. People were rushing up and down the now brightly lit sidewalks, and cars passed by in a hurried fashion.

"Don't believe it, do ya? Well, see for yourself. Take out your phone and call or text someone," insisted Eckerd.

"I don't have a cell phone," Joseph replied. The reporter resisted technology at all costs. Not that he was opposed to it; he rather preferred getting things done the old-fashioned way and avoiding distraction, social media, and a constant barrage of phone calls, emails, and texts. He tried to avoid anything that would chain him to his electronic device. Joseph believed it was better to look up and see the world for what it was than to look down at a device in a world that did not really exist, a world filled with facades.

"Well, if you don't have a phone, you will just have to take my word for it. So, what will it be? What flavor of gelato would you like?"

"I will keep to my favorite—old-fashioned vanilla, please," requested the reporter, now more relaxed.

"Sorry, we're out. Pick something else please," came the reply from

Eckerd.

"Fine, make it chocolate."

Once again, Eckerd was quick to refuse his order. "Sorry, we're out of that as well."

At this point, Joseph was suspicious. He could see both requested flavors in cartons behind the glass of the freezer.

"What if I were to ask you for the salted caramel?"

Eckerd's face revealed a look of satisfaction.

"I was beginning to think you would never ask." All at once an intense tremor began to shake beneath their feet. The lights overhead dimmed and flickered for a moment then suddenly where once stood the back interior wall, now an open doorway leading into a back room appeared.

"Curious parlor trick, Eckerd," Joseph said, looking alarmed. "Let me guess, you probably want me to go in that room, correct?"

The lederhosen-clad man didn't say a word. He bowed his upper body and extended out his left arm suggesting to Joseph to enter the room.

Being a reporter, Joseph had often found himself in peculiar situations that made him uncomfortable and unsure of his safety. This situation was different, however as he was in a perplexing situation, though he did not sense any danger. Assessing the situation once more and feeling propelled by his own unquenchable curiosity, he walked cautiously through the doorway.

The room was slightly dilapidated yet warm. Evidence of a neglected, underused room covered the antique corner tables in a thick layer of dust. This room was dimly lit, receiving its only light from the glow of the embers burning in a stone fireplace to the rear of the room. From the corner of the room, a wooden chair and a worn, overstuffed red leather armchair were visible. A paunchy silhouette of a man could be seen resting in his throne-like seat. The flames from the fire cast a haunting, dim light on the man. Gazing across the room, Joseph could make out the man's well-groomed snow-white beard with multiple ringlets mixed with silky waves of hair that cascaded down his face like a waterfall off a mountainside. His magnificent facial hair was full and covered the man's thick neck and colossal upper chest. His beard was indeed the center focus of the man and adorned him like a proud lion strutting around with a thick mane.

"Please come in closer, dear lad," a gentle voice said from the red chair in the corner. Joseph stepped cautiously closer to the man and stopped when he approached a wooden chair that had been placed in the middle of the room next to a small round table lamp. From this distance, Joseph judged that this was a man filled with years of experience, know-how, and wisdom all wrapped up in an ever-aging body. The deep lines emanating from the corners of his eyes suggested he was likely in his mid-seventies. A subtle, thin, two-inch vertical scar over his right cheekbone told a story of a previous trauma years ago, though it had softened with time. On his nose rested polished gold-framed bifocals that magnified his deep blue eyes and oversized pupils.

"Please, sit down and rest." The large man pointed toward the wooden chair in front of Joseph. "I'm sure you have grown weary from your journey."

The soft-spoken words comforted the reporter, and he obliged in following the directions without speaking a word back.

"I appreciate you taking time away from your busy schedule to meet me. I have long pondered what to say when we would meet. I have also contemplated several times foregoing this interview, fearing the time was not right," explained the man. "Good heavens, where are my manners? Mr. Amesbury, I have watched you for years and have read your work in the *Gazette*. In my personal opinion, you're simply the best and most accomplished reporter I have come to learn about." The plump man stretched out his thick right hand in a gesture of greeting. "My name is Kristoff Nikolaus Christkindl, and it's a real pleasure to meet you."

"Likewise." Joseph stood up, extended his right arm, and grasped Mr. Christkindl's soft, chubby hand, giving it a firm handshake. "The pleasure is all mine, sir."

The reporter sat back in his chair, analyzing the name presented to him. "You say your last name is Christkindl? I have heard that name before," he continued. "Supposedly, this name had been mispronounced in the past and had been interpreted as KRINGLE."

"Oh, yes," came the reply from Kristoff. "Kringle is what they called me back in the war. Joseph, I brought you here tonight because I desire to make a Solemn declaration to the world. I want it to be known to you and to all that will read your article that my name is Kristoff Nikolaus Christkindl, or the very same man known as Kris Kringle."

"Wait a moment!" Joseph interrupted. "Are you telling me, or claiming to the world that you are that jolly ol' man, Father Christmas, even THE Santa Claus?"

Mr. Christkindl's eyes narrowed as he stared directly at Joseph. "I have been referred to by many names, but to answer your question, yes, this is what I declare to the world, you as my witness."

Joseph was always quick when under pressure and portrayed confidence even when he didn't feel it. After a brief silent pause that felt like an eternity, Joseph felt once again confident and solid in his thoughts. "May I inquire as to your former place of residence? Dare I say Berlin?" Asking this question bought Joseph enough time to process what this elderly man was claiming. *Claiming to know magic or magic tricks is one thing, but to claim yourself to be a magical creature of folklore is over-the-top barmy, and completely insane!*

A deafening silence filled the room as both men sat across from one another like two people dueling it out over a game of chess. The creak of the wood floor chased away the quietude of the room. Eckerd entered carrying a silver serving platter covered with a large oval lid. He gently placed the platter down on the small round table nearest to Joseph.

Eckerd snapped to attention while standing next to the sitting reporter, awaiting further instructions from Mr. Christkindl.

"I know you might find it difficult, if not impossible to believe my claims. However, I promise that if you give me your time and attention, you will see things more clearly than ever. You will discover my deepest magical secrets and learn the answer to life's longest questions regarding me. I assure you, this will be the biggest and most widely read article ever printed by the *Gazette*."

Mr. Amesbury settled deeper in his chair and considered the pudgy man's offer. "Joseph," the jolly old man said in a subdued yet respectful tone, "I think you would feel better with a bit of food in your stomach. It may help you see things more clearly."

Mr. Christkindl glanced down at the silver platter sitting on the coffee table next to the reporter, then looked toward Eckerd. Dipping his head forward and back, he gave a slight nod to his assistant standing in the room. In one swift motion, Eckerd reached down, grasped the oval lid covering the platter, and removed it. Steam vapors wafted upward, revealing sausages and potatoes garnishing the plate. "I thought you might enjoy this entrée, Joseph," Kristoff said. I had Eckerd prepare it before your arrival. After all, it is one of your favorite dishes if my long observations of you have been correct. Good ol' bangers and mash.

4

A Distant Memory

The savory sausages and seasoned potatoes melted in the reporter's mouth, filling his vacant stomach with each delicious bite. "Well, Mr. Christkindl, I am grateful for the delightful meal, and I must say, I am highly intrigued by what you said about observing me and how you knew about my favorite dish. You definitely deserve my attention, and I have several questions for you regarding your claim of being Santa."

"Right then. So, let's begin," the incredulous reporter insisted. "How old are you? Where were you born? Do you really have a house full of elves?"

"Slow down there." Mr. Christkindl chuckled quietly. "I know you have many questions. If you are to appreciate all I have to say, you must stop asking questions and let the answers precede the questions. If you are patient, the story unravels itself." Checking to see the reporter's response, Mr. Christkindl continued, "Like it's stated in the Bible, dear Joseph, line upon line, here a little, and there a little. All will be answered.

"I was born in Germany in the year 1922. My mother Elsa—"

"Wait, wait, wait…that doesn't add up!" interrupted Mr. Amesbury.

"I thought Santa was supposed to be much older than that! Are you claiming to have been born in 1922 even though the story claims he has been around for centuries?"

"Well, the Santa as you have come to know, or the legend, has been around for many centuries; this is a true statement," Mr. Christkindl said respectfully. "Patience, antsy lad, patience. It will all be as clear as melted icicles before you know it," he calmly stated.

"My apologies. It was a real cock up interrupting you like that. Very unprofessional."

"No apology needed," Kristoff replied. "Besides, it can only be expected when everything you have been told by society is laced with fact and intermingled with fiction.

"As I was saying, I was born in Germany in 1922. My mother, Elsa, named me after my maternal grandfather Kristof Schultz. Our Schultz family tree can be traced deep into German history. However, my mother's family moved to England two generations ago. Mother was always proud of her German heritage and the family continued to speak German in the home. However, she learned English over the years. Being a God-fearing woman, my mother gave me the middle name of Nikolaus, named after Saint Nikolaus of Myra, the fourth-century Christian saint.

"It just so happened that my father's name was also Nikolaus, so it was easy to convince my father that I should keep his name. Mother felt that giving me the name of an honorable man like my father and St. Nikolaus might influence me for good and inspire me to seek after the poor and the needy. My father was also German, and his Kringle family line can be traced further back in history than the Schultz family tree."

Kristoff stood up and made his way to a white porcelain candy dish sitting on top of the antique corner table. Stuffing his chubby fingers inside, he retrieved a chocolate truffle and popped it in his mouth. "Oh, how I love a smooth truffle. Besides, we all need a little sugar pick-me-up now and then," he said with a slight chuckle.

Kristoff returned to his seat and rested his elbows on the armrests. "Sadly, my mother became a widow at an early age when I was only five years old and never remarried. I kept the surname of Kringle for some time, but being called Kristoff Kringle or Kris Kringle as my friends called me made me an easy target at school. I don't think my mother saw it coming. Anyways, I did abandon my Kringle name during the war and took on Christkindl in its place. It has been with me ever since."

Joseph placed his pencil and paper down on the floor next to him, leaned back in his chair, and crossed his right leg over his left. Tilting his head slightly forward, he stared intently at the bearded man sitting across from him.

"When I was just a little boy, I was told that my father had been killed in a work-related accident at a factory in Berlin. Mother was heartbroken by the sudden loss of her sweetheart and told me later in my life that she had needed to get far away from Berlin after his death. The reminder of her tragic loss resurfaced each time she would look out her window and see the factory tower where her husband had worked. Being a young widow, she needed to start a new life for the two of us, so she moved us to the outskirts of Munich and took up a job as a seamstress at a local men's clothing shop downtown. I still remember that day, the day when I met my best friend...."

"Mama, must I go with you to work today?" the eight-year-old Kristoff complained.

"I have no place to leave you while I am away to work," his mother said. "Besides, they have a lovely daughter about your age. Perhaps you might play together."

"Das Mädchen? A girl? You want me to play with a girl? Forget it!" the young Kristoff protested.

"Oh, Kris, give it a chance. Girls can be a lot of fun. You like playing games with me, and after all, I used to be a little girl too, you know."

The two of them giggled at her comment as they continued down the sidewalk hand in hand.

Kristoff's mother, Elsa, was a slender brunette with shoulder-length wavy hair and a heart-shaped face. Her eyes were a majestic emerald green that stood out against her soft olive skin and her straight-edged nose that turned up slightly at the end. Her striking appearance caused many men to turn and stare at her as they passed her on the sidewalk, even on the busiest days. Her father was of stern German blood, and her mother was a British immigrant to Germany who was very proper and caring.

Elsa had inherited her father's square chin, thin lips, and unwavering determination to have success in all that she did, including raising Kristoff as a single mother. She did a remarkable job caring for her son and was prompt to encourage him when at times things did not go the way he had hoped. She would often tell him in his moments of frustration that we learn from our mistakes. Elsa seemed to always have the right words to lift his spirits and put a smile back on his face.

Her mother's attributes were manifest in Elsa through her caring nature for others, a soft-spoken mannerism, and her ability to speak the English language, though her father had insisted they speak German in the home. Elsa grew up appreciating different cultures, languages, and the gift of communicating with others. As a grown woman and mother, she was bound and determined that her son Kristoff also learn a second language and ensured it by speaking to him both in English and German since the time of his birth. She felt it was important to pass on this heritage and did her part to see to it that he would be proficient in both languages.

At length, they arrived at a small clothing store with a mannequin displaying a dark suit behind the front store's glass window with the name Blumenfeld painted in yellow lettering with a dark green outline. "All right then, Kris, this is the place. Now remember your manners and be on your best behavior!" she instructed her son.

"I will, Mama. You can count on me."

Elsa pushed open the front door, whacking a small brass bell above it. High-pitched chimes rattled from the bell while it danced around wildly from the impact of the heavy door. In a flash, the two entering patrons were greeted hastily by the eager owner.

"Guten Morgen!" A short, balding man with round spectacles approached them from behind a counter. "Hello there, little boy. I'm Alfred Blumenfeld, and this is my wife Martha," he said, pointing to the middle-aged woman with ginger hair to his left.

Kristoff thrust his hand forward and clasped the man's hand, giving it a firm shake. "Pleased to meet you, sir," said Kristoff. "My name is Kristoff Kringle, and I am eight years old."

Alfred chuckled as he shook Kristoff's hand. "Well, aren't you the proper young man!" he exclaimed. "Right this way, if you please," Mr. Blumenfeld said as he led them to the back of the store.

Mrs. Blumenfeld handed Elsa an apron and guided her to the tailoring station. "Right over here, dear," she said. "You will be working with me at this table. I will show you the ropes."

"I have some training in this area, Mrs. Blumenfeld. My mother was a tailor," Elsa said humbly.

"Good to know! You will fit right in," she replied with a smile.

Mr. Blumenfeld motioned Kristoff to the corner of the room, where a small girl was tidying up some odds and ends. "Lorelei, dear, please come meet our guests. This is Mrs. Kringle and her young son Kristoff," he announced.

Lorelei ran her palms over the front of her dress in a sweeping motion and then wiped her hands on the sides of her gown before extending one hand to shake with Kristoff. "Pleased to meet you, Kristoff," she said with a grin. Lorelei had curly blonde hair tied up in pigtails and deep blue eyes. Her cheeks were round and full of color, and her smile revealed a small dimple on her left cheek. She wore a dark blue dress with white trim and buttons down the front. Her shoes were a shiny black and polished to perfection. It was obvious that Lorelei was very involved with the family business and did her fair share of the work around the house.

"Pleased to meet you, Lorelei. Mum has told me loads about you."

"That is wonderful news. She is less of a stranger to you then," Mr. Blumenfeld said. "Now that you have been formally introduced, Lorelei, why don't you show Kristoff around?" he instructed.

"Very well, Papa," came her reply. "Follow me, Kristoff. Now that we are friends, it's best that I show you the best places to play."

Kristoff was puzzled about the instant friendship that was being proclaimed by this young girl. As far as Kristoff was concerned, a friendship needs time to develop. However, he was new to the neighborhood, and after all, he needed someone his own age to talk to. At this point, there was no way around it. With his juvenile logic, he lowered his "boys only" pride and welcomed Lorelei into his circle of friends. "Right then. Show me around," he said.

Lorelei was a fast runner and did not waste any time demonstrating this to her new friend. She ran to the back of the store and up the wooden staircase that hugged the back wall. Kristoff was also athletic, and keeping up with a girl was a must. He gave it his best effort, but grudgingly he admitted to himself, she was indeed faster than him.

The two children reached the top of the stairs, and Lorelei told Kristoff to stop where he stood. Kristoff stared at her, awaiting further instruction. "Raise your right hand!" came her command.

"Why?" asked Kristoff.

"You must swear to secrecy before I can let you take another step."

"Secrecy about what?" asked Kristoff.

"Secrecy of the hidden opening to my hideaway," she answered.

"Very well, get on with it," he replied.

"Raise your right hand!" she insisted once again.

Kristoff raised his right arm up to his side and formed a square angle with the palm of his hand facing forward. "Like this?"

"Perfect," came her reply. "Now repeat after me: I, Kristoff, swear on my mother's grave—"

"But my mother is still alive, Lorelei."

"Don't interrupt!" she insisted. "Go on, repeat after me: I, Kristoff, swear on my mother's grave that I will never tell anyone the location of the secret opening to Lorelei's hideaway."

Kristoff reluctantly repeated every word. When he finished, Lorelei spat in her hand and bade Kristoff to spit in his. Kristoff recognized that this was the token of a sealed deal, spat in his hand, and grabbed Lorelei's hand, giving it a solid shake. The two children giggled when they completed the agreement.

Lorelei wiped the spit from her hand onto her dress, then dropped to her knees and crawled slowly to the corner of the room. Kristoff could not see exactly what she was doing. However, he noted she was tugging up on the wooden floorboard a short distance from where Kristoff stood. With some effort, she removed a small section of the wooden floor and slipped down into the exposed opening.

"Kristoff, come quick. Follow me," she said.

Uncertain as to what awaited him, he mimicked her by crawling on the floor to the excavated section of the flooring. Peering over the edge revealed a small opening between the ceiling of the department store and the flooring of the attic.

"Wow, this is amazing," he exclaimed. Though the area was small, it was large enough to sit up in comfortably and contained several items that had been stored away. A small-framed family portrait was propped up next to a wooden crate, which was full of stored dry foods and sealed tin cans. Many liquid-filled vessels with the word "wasser" hand-painted in white lettering on them sat near the food. A small metal plate, cup, spoon, and a tiny can opener were also there. A small stack of blankets, a pillow, and a small cigar box that was tied up with packaging string completed the inventory.

"This is marvelous. How did you ever find this place and get these things up here, Lorelei?"

"I didn't," she said. "My father made it for me. He told me if there ever is a time to hide, this is where I should do it."

"Why would you need to hide?" Kristoff asked.

"I don't know for certain. He tells me the world is changing, Germany is changing, and we can't be certain of our future here. Father always talks to my mother about a Nazi group leader named … I can't remember his name, but I remember he was previously imprisoned and now leads a group of people called Nazis. My dad said some scary things about him and wants to make sure I am always safe. He built this for me and told me not to tell anyone about it. I haven't, until today, with you. You must keep this secret! I insist, Kristoff. Never tell anyone."

Kristoff nodded his head in affirmation. "I promise, Lorelei. Your secret is safe with me."

Downstairs, the front door brass bell chimed excitedly again, alerting them of another visitor. "Sounds like Father is busy. Come let me show you what he does for work." Lorelei and Kristoff carefully replaced the wooden flooring and bounded down the staircase and out of sight, leaving the hide-out in the attic behind.

5

The Sealed Deal

The emergence of this friendship soon became a distant memory as the next several years drifted away as fast as dreams dissolve in the morning light. Kristoff and Lorelei became inseparable in their many adventures, family outings, and work at the store. The two were so frequently seen together that they eventually became the center of gossip at the local beauty shop. Kristoff's affections for Lorelei deepened over the years, and he often wanted to tell her he loved her. However, his boyhood embarrassment kept him silent. Every time he tried to muster the courage, the words choked in his throat, leaving him speechless. Instead, he would wink his left eye at her at the end of their visits. Lorelei must have understood the mutual meaning behind his wink because her cheeks would flush a warm pink that complemented her soft red lips.

The year was now 1938, and Lorelei had just celebrated her sixteenth birthday. Kristoff was a few months younger than her and would soon be turning sixteen. Lorelei's blonde hair had darkened only slightly over the years. She would often pull back her sun-bleached golden locks into a tight ponytail. At the age of eleven, Kristoff passed Lorelei in height and was now revealing his maturing body with muscular arms and powerful legs. His boyish soft features had gradually sharpened into a squared-off jawline, high cheekbones, and his voice was now a full octave lower than the other young men in his grade.

Over the years, Lorelei had excelled in her scholastic achievements and became an excellent student, often boasting of her superior grades to Kristoff. She was better in all subjects at school except one: biology. Kristoff never studied for his biology exams. He could always solve the problems on exams by simple deduction and dissecting the question down into a simple process of elimination. For reasons unknown to him, he took to science like a duck to water and rarely walked away from an exam with less than a perfect score. Biology had always been exciting to him, and he often stayed after school just to read more about science in his textbooks. More often than not, his instructors would insist that he head home so they could depart the school grounds.

One particular Saturday morning, Kristoff's mother, Elsa, had risen a bit earlier to prepare a fine breakfast for her growing young man. Kristoff was still in a deep sleep from staying up late the night before and was oblivious to the banging of pans, skillets, or her business in the kitchen. Elsa had something very important on her mind today that she wanted to discuss with her son and wanted to create the perfect setting for such a conversation. She knew the subject matter was a tender one and wanted to set the appropriate environment.

What better way to put a growing boy in a pleasant mood than to prepare her son's favorite meal, she thought. Her son loved to indulge in crispy bacon, savory sausages, and warm creamy yolk eggs, and he would eat them any hour of the day if allowed. He never seemed to grow tired of them. Being a sixteen-year-old boy, Kristoff often felt his growing body needed twelve hours of sleep each night. The daily morning routine to wake him up was extremely consistent and slightly comical to observe. Often his mother would be forced to pry him out of his bed, especially on Saturday mornings, by any means available to her. Kristoff was known to roll over in his bed and pull his pillow hard over his head in an attempt to block any ray of sunlight that may possibly penetrate his tightly closed eyelids and would request just one more minute of sleep from his mother.

Unfortunately, this one minute became two, then twenty, and by and by an additional hour would pass before she would be forced to take additional persuasive tactics. It had been known to the neighbors living above them that he had been awoken with a glass of cold water tossed on him in his bed more than on one occasion. The acute water awakening strategy to roost her slumbering son from his bed was often accompanied by a high-pitched pubescent voice screaming out, "Mama, no, not wasser again!"

Today was different from most Saturday mornings. This time Elsa ensured that Kristoff was well rested and in a mood to reason with. The aroma of cooked bacon wafted its way through the small one-bedroom home and found its way into the flared nares of her sleeping adolescent. Twitching lips and several whiffs from his wrinkled nose confirmed he was indeed smelling the scented alarm clock his mother had fried up in the kitchen.

"Mama, is that bacon I smell?" he questioned.

"Ja, Sohn. Yes, son, it is," she replied.

"Speck! I love speck. How did you do it, Mama? We cannot afford bacon." He was now fully alert and full of concern.

"Kristoff, this is not for you to worry about. Just know that I have been able to save a little money so I can make a proper breakfast for an amazing son. Now don't waste time and let it get cold," Elsa said. "Come quickly to the table and let's give thanks for the food we have."

In an instant, Kristoff was out of bed and racing to the table where several darkened strips of bacon garnished two fried eggs and a soft biscuit with butter. This was a very special meal indeed, and different from the bread and marmalade they would often have for breakfast.

"I don't understand, Mama. My birthday has passed. Why bacon and eggs?"

"Kristoff, enjoy the food before it gets cold."

Breakfast was a delight and a special treat compared to the warm mush they so often would eat. The meager income from working at the Blumenfeld suit shop gave barely enough money for their room and board. Living below their means was the secret to survival with such a limited income or resources. The two sat together enjoying the salty bacon and lapping up the runny yolk of the fried egg with a warm biscuit. However, because Kristoff was still trying to wake up, the conversation at the table was limited to only a few words of gratitude to his mother for the breakfast. During the entire meal, Kristoff stared down at the small porcelain plate as if studying abstract art made by the streaks of drying yolk left behind.

His mother was a bit subdued, and the look on her face told a story that something concerned her. It appeared she was unsure how to initiate the conversation. The deafening silence was interrupted by the clattering of dirty dishes being scrubbed by his mother, who was now standing at the sink. Kristoff stood up and joined in the cleaning by clearing the remaining dishes and wiping down the well-worn wooden table. He always helped his mother around the house and was generally a step ahead to alleviate the need for her to ask him for help. He felt that it was his duty to honor his mother and help with any necessary tasks. The way he saw it, his mother worked hard to support him, and he wanted to work hard to serve her back. With the kitchen table cleaned off, Kristoff thanked his mother once again, and excused himself so he could go meet up with Lorelei.

"Please sit for a minute, Kristoff, before you go visit Lorelei," Elsa insisted. "I have something of an important matter to discuss with you."

Kristoff sat down, and Elsa sat across the table from him once again.

However, this time she reached out her hands and grasped both of her son's hands gently. Her brilliant green eyes stared directly into his, and by degrees, the words began to fall into place. "Kris, what I will ask of you may be hard to hear. I have thought this through, and I feel that the time has come to ask. As you know, I do care for Lorelei, and I often think of her as family. She has certainly become a dear friend of yours."

"Mama, I'm not ready to marry her yet," Kristoff blurted out.

Elsa, slightly taken back, continued, "Well, I'm not asking you to take her hand in marriage, Kris."

Kristoff was slightly embarrassed and felt his cheeks flush.

"What I'm going to ask of you may be the hardest thing I have ever felt impressed to have you do."

Kristoff felt puzzled. "What is it, Mama? What would you have me do?"

Elsa's eyes narrowed. "Kris, I know you have been taunted relentlessly and together we have avoided you joining the Hitlerjugend. But I feel impressed that you must join as soon as possible."

"Mama, you must be joking with me. I will not join that Hitler youth group of haters!" Kristoff raised his voice in alarm.

"Kris, hear me out. I have been talking with Mr. Blumenfeld, and he fears that in time Hitler and the Nazi party will increase their attacks on the Jewish people. Just last week, Mr. Blumenfeld's cousin was taken to a camp outside of the city and he has not been heard of since. He now fears the safety of his family, and especially Lorelei. Perhaps by joining this group, you may help gather vital information regarding the Jews, Nazi plans, and potentially help prevent any harm that may come our way or even attacks on the Blumenfeld family."

Kristoff lowered his head in contemplation. The room fell deathly still, and an uneasy silence filled his ears. Elsa stood up, went to the counter, and commenced wiping the biscuit crumbs from it with her soggy dishrag. Kristoff continued to sit, rapidly tapping his index finger on the tabletop, his rage festering inside of him with every rotation of the minute hand on the clock. The thought of joining the very group that wanted to inflict harm on his best friend was more than he could stomach. Jumping out of his chair, he stormed out of the house and down the street to cool off.

I need time to think. I need to clear my head, he thought. Unlocking the front door to the house, he thundered down the busy sidewalk dodging the rush of morning pedestrians marching toward their places of employment. Kristoff's brown leather shoes slapped the concrete with every frustrated step, the store fronts passed him on either side in a streaking blur. Pent up anger inside fueled his exodus as he continued to distance himself from his home for several city blocks. His lungs swelled to capacity with every gulp of air, and his heart thundered in his chest as he continued to push himself, testing his endurance.

By and by, and block after block, his pace slowed to a steady comfortable stroll. The cool humid air of the morning helped extinguish his burning lungs, and the scent of the damp grass filled his nostrils. His frustration of being asked to join the Hitlerjugend melted away from the endorphins released from his sprint across town, when suddenly his body was slammed from behind.

He catapulted into the air, landing in a twisted mess upon the city park lawn. His right shoulder smashed into the trunk of a mature alder tree, and his left arm was flailed out to his side, attempting to stop his fall. Thick mud smashed between his teeth. Pressure surged over his right kidney and inflicted pain with every passing second. Reaching behind him with his right arm, he grasped the object pressing down on his lower back. To his astonishment, it was not an automobile, a bicycle, or even a metal thing at all. It was the warm, soft, recognizable sensation of skin— a knee was pressing down on his back. *Oh no*, he worried. *My leg, I cannot feel my own leg. How on earth Is my leg contorted and pressing down on my back?*

A small grunt of pain was interrupted by an ever-increasing laugh. Soon the laughter was so intense that a familiar snort emanated from behind him.

"Lorelei, you're killing me. Get off my back!" Kristoff grumbled. "Was that you that tackled me? What were you thinking?"

Lorelei's eyes widened. "I called out to you when you started running away from your home. I kept calling out to you, but you never turned around, so I continued to chase. I know I am faster than you, and, honestly, I didn't want to run all morning long behind you, so I planned my attack at the first sight of grass." Picking moist dirt out of Kristoff's eyebrow, she continued, "And now here we are. Tell me, Kristoff, why are you running? Where are you off to?"

Kristoff shrugged his shoulders. "Where to start is the real question," he said sarcastically. "Well, it started over eggs, and bacon…."

The two youth flopped down on a cool patch of grass under the shade of the aged alder tree Kristoff had smashed into, and he rehearsed the morning's events in its entirety, of course, leaving out the part about thinking that his mom wanted him to marry Lorelei. He was much too embarrassed to let her know his fondness for her, much too guarded to let go of his heart at this point in his life, though often he had admitted to himself that she was his only world, his life, and at times the reason he couldn't wait to wake up in the mornings.

"Gosh, Kristoff, this is terrible indeed. I think I understand why you were running away from your house this morning."

"Yeah, I knew you would be able to understand, Lorelei."

"There is, however, one thing I don't quite understand about you, Kristoff," she said. "Why do you run so slowly?"

"Oh, you didn't just say that!" Kristoff said, then he lunged forward in an attempt to grab her.

The two jumped to their feet and darted through the park, in a sort of cat and mouse game. It was clear that Lorelei was the faster sprinter and enjoyed the fact that she was being chased by Kristoff, even though she clearly had the advantage over him. She would purposely slow down just enough to be barely out of reach of his outstretched fingers and then accelerate in a sudden burst of energy leaving Kristoff empty handed. Lorelei had amazing agility and her next move made it obvious that she really wanted to be captured. All at once, she came to an abrupt stop, turned on her heels, and faced her opponent.

With determination in his eyes, Kristoff softened his tackle and gracefully lowered his best friend down to the ground. Kristoff stared deeply into her eyes but did not say a word. He could feel his chest rising and falling quickly as he tried to catch his breath from the rapid chase. Lorelei broke eye contact and was now staring at Kristoff's flushed lips.

"You win, Kristoff. Now claim your reward." The invitation came with a slight nervous giggle.

Kristoff, as if driven by an unseen force, leaned in close, and with all the tenderness he possessed, pressed his lips to hers. A feeling of warmth flooded his entire body like a warm blanket wrapping him up on a winter's morning. He could hear his heart pounding in his ears. In a split second, he thought, *What just happened? What did I just do?*

This was something that was not planned. Up to this moment, Kristoff had not entertained the idea of kissing a girl, especially kissing his very best friend, Lorelei. The clumsy smooch made it obvious that this was indeed the first time he had ever kissed a girl, and judging by the look on Lorelei's blushing face, this was the first time she was a kiss recipient.

The moment ended as quickly as it started. If anyone had witnessed it, they would say that it wasn't more than a peck on the lips. But that didn't matter, it didn't need to be a long drawn-out kiss. It was long enough to seal the emotions and create a new depth of his relationship with Lorelei.

The two did not say a word to one another right away after the kiss. Both were unsure what to say or even how to say it. For that brief moment following the kiss, and though they had spent every day together for many years, it felt like they had just met for the first time. Kristoff gently helped Lorelei to her feet and helped her brush off the thick blades of grass sticking to the back of her shirt.

Turning away from the park, there was a new unsaid understanding in the air surrounding the young couple as they began walking back in the direction they had been running from. The quiet stroll back toward their homes began to eat at Lorelei so much that she decided to break the thick silence by discussing Kristoff's mother's proposal to join the Hitler youth group.

"You know, Kristoff," she said, her soft voice breaking the awkwardness, "perhaps your mother is right. Joining this group may be a way to keep us informed of ongoing events with the German military as well as help my family be safe from harm's way. This whole thing scares me to be honest with you. I am so concerned about what could happen to me or my family in the future." Lorelei looked down at her leg and flicked off a chunk of soil and grass still sticking to her. "Hopefully this whole messy thing will all just pass over and be forgotten. I find myself so worried about it and the many changes we have seen in Germany these past few months that I actually have trouble sleeping at night. Just to think, all of this is pressed upon us just because of our religion." Lorelei sighed. "I believe in you, Kris. You are a very strong person, and I know you will be a great asset to us. Perhaps joining the Hitlerjugend is the right thing after all."

Kristoff stopped in his tracks and sat down on the street curb. A street sign towering above him blocked out just enough of the morning sun to cast a thin shadow on his concrete make-shift seat. Lorelei stopped and joined him on the curb taking advantage of the shadow to block the intense sun rays from shining in her eyes.

"This is a hard thing for me to do, Lorelei." Kristoff dropped his head in frustration. "I love the Jewish people. I love all people. I love you,

Lorelei."

That awkward feeling was back in an instant, his stomach stirring with butterflies. Disclosing to Lorelei that he loved her sort of dribbled out of his mouth like a pudgy boy indulging in a mouthful of ice cream too big to swallow and the cream seeping out the corner of his lips.

Lorelei slightly blushed from what she had just heard. "You must promise me to do this, Kristoff," she insisted.

Kristoff closed his eyes tightly. "Fine, I will do it. I will join the Hitlerjugend. However, you must listen to me, Lorelei, and do exactly as I tell you when I gather information that may prevent attacks on you or on any of the Jewish community, for that matter."

Lorelei stretched her hand forward to bind the deal by a handshake. "Kristoff, one more thing," she said, her tone now more direct. "You must do whatever you can to prevent giving away your true loyalties to both me and the Jewish people. You must keep your secret safe, even if it may place me in a tough situation. You know, if they suspect you to be a traitor, they may hurt you, or perhaps, possibly something much worse." With her side of the deal declared, Kristoff looked down at the palm of his right hand and spit in it. In one sweeping motion, he reached forward, grabbed her hand, and sealed the deal, just like he had done so many years ago in the attic above her father's store.

6

The Night of Broken Glass

Several months had passed since that morning in the city park, and since that time, Lorelei and Kristoff's relationship naturally matured and the feelings for one another continued to deepen and blossom. Neither youth had been in a boyfriend-girlfriend relationship before, and this relationship was even more difficult to navigate since they had to keep it secret from others in order to protect one another.

In recent events, Kristoff had agreed to the persuasions of his mother and Lorelei and reluctantly joined the Hitler youth group using his Kringle name to prove his long German lineage. Upon joining the Hitlerjugend, he found favor with the recruiting personnel, and in time was able to convince them to use Christkindl as his last name in place of Kringle to avoid jeers from the fellow youth. The renamed Christkindl spent many evenings attending meetings and rallies in his new military uniform as well as participating in training exercises for the Hitlerjugend.

At length Kristoff discovered that the training was very physical in nature and included agility tests, weapons training, and military tactics.

It was the aim of the Nazi party to train this group of youth to become faithful members of the Nazi party, who at some point, may become future Nazi party leaders.

Kristoff did prove well in the training and achieved top marks on target shooting in both handguns and the long rifle events. More often than not, he had also found himself finishing first in the physical training courses because of his large stature and strength, even though he was only sixteen years of age.

Besides the intense military training, Kristoff also received a constant barrage of anti-Jewish literature and Nazi indoctrination at the weekly meetings and scheduled rallies. These weekly meeting were always taught by adults and the lessons about racial purity and anti-Semitism would make his blood boil with anger. It became increasingly difficult for him not to stand up and rebuke the lecturer. He and the other youth were being force-fed racism and hatred toward the Jewish community. It took all of the strength he could muster to keep his composure and not accidently give away his true loyalties and the real reason for joining the Hitlerjugend.

The persecutions of the Jewish people continued to escalade in intensity making it steadily more difficult for Lorelei and Kristoff to spend time together. The playground where the two had spent so much time as children, as well as the community pool, no longer permitted Jewish people to enter. The two of them first noticed these new changes months prior when Lorelei was not allowed to enter a museum merely because she was a Jewish girl. The experience was awful because the two had planned a Saturday morning together only to be told at the door that the "dirty Jewish girl" was not permitted in the museum and told Kristoff to drag her back to her neighborhood where she belonged. Tears streamed down Lorelei's cheeks as she and Kristoff walked away from the stone building trying to wrap their heads around what had just happened.

The weekly Hitlerjugend meetings did serve their purpose, however, for Kristoff and on more than one occasion he informed specific families of impending attacks. It was a reward to him to warn the families and later hear from frustrated leaders that the targeted families had suddenly packed up and left before the SS could inflict any harm or make arrests.

Today's Hitlerjugend meeting was different from previous meetings. Rather than physical exercise and typical Nazi indoctrination, there was an announcement made by Herr Schirach. His hatred towards the Jewish community was felt as he proudly read a report delivered to him earlier that morning. Herr Schirach loudly cleared his voice, demanding everyone's attention.

"Today, the ninth day of November 1938, I wish to read you part of a telegraph I received. Nearly seventeen thousand Polish Jews have been expelled from Germany and we have forced them to the Polish border. Poland is refusing to take them, and they are now in a sort of no-man's-land between Germany and Poland, near the town of Zbaszyn." He read the note with a snake-like smile. "Now the filth are homeless, hungry, and, with any luck, will starve to death."

A snicker came from a greasy, dark-haired, skinny boy named Gunter, sitting in the front row. Kristoff felt his fingernails digging into the undersurface of the wooden desk he was sitting in. His anger was fueled by what he was hearing and Gunter's reaction. He was now at boiling point.

"My dear Jungen, I have received some tragic news in which I have been instructed to inform you of." Herr Schirach lowered his head in an act of respect and mourning. "It has come to my attention that two days ago a seventeen-year-old Polish Jew who was living in Paris shot Ernst vom Rath, our diplomat attached to the German embassy in Paris. Ernst vom Rath passed away today, after two days of suffering in pain. This filthy Jewish boy claims that he did this horrible act because his parents are trapped along with other Polish Jews in the no-man's-land

I have just told you about. This criminal did not act alone in an isolated outburst of rage, but this is part of a wider Jewish conspiracy against Germany." Herr Schirach now shouted at them like he himself had seen the Führer do at previous military meetings.

Gunter Müller stood up in the front row. He turned around, revealing his crooked nose, and shouted, "What is to be done to rid us of these Jews! I hate them! I hate them all!" The room went still, and silence replaced the elevated voice of their leader.

Herr Schirach walked over to Gunter and placed his hand on the boy's shoulder. "Sit down, my dear Gunter. I understand your devotion to the Führer, and I share your hatred of the Jews. I have something that you can do, something you can do to help the Führer accomplish his cleansing of the Jews from the earth. I have received intelligence that tonight we are to enter the city and destroy their buildings and houses and inflict all manner of fear in the Jewish community. Unfortunately, I have also been instructed that you are not to kill them, only to kill their spirit of living. Cause them to leave, and if they don't go, lock them up and escort them to the camps we have prepared for them."

Kristoff, alarmed by this news, stood up in protest, knocking over his chair. His tight fists were shaking at his side, though he did not shout a word.

Herr Schirach whipped his head around and stared intensely at Kristoff. "What is this? Standing up for the Jews?" he lashed out at him.

Kristoff had not realized that he had stood up. "No, sir. I'm just eager to destroy the Jewish property and assist our Führer in his purification."

Schirach's demeanor changed. He looked into Kristoff's eyes, examining them. "You will get your chance tonight to prove your loyalties."

Kristoff sat back down and noted Gunter glaring at him from the front row. "If you ask me, I think Kristoff loves the Jews. In fact, I hear he has a Jewish girlfriend."

"That will be enough, Gunter. Turn around." Herr Schirach continued to give instructions. The leader's voice was quickly drowned out of Kristoff's ears by the thoughts racing inside of his head.

What of the Blumenfeld suit shop? What of Mr. and Mrs. Blumenfeld? Oh my gosh, what of Lorelei? he thought in a desperate panic. *I must get to the Blumenfelds!*

The meeting adjourned, and each Hitler Youth fled to prepare for the night's event. Kristoff bolted down the street, but before he could reach the end, he was tackled by Gunter and two of his buddies, Hanz Bauer and Adolf Schmitt.

"Running off to see your Jewish girlfriend?" asked Gunter.

"I don't know what you are talking about," Kristoff said.

"Oh, come on now, Kristoff," Hanz, a short strawberry-blond boy with multiple pimples speckling his face, said. "We have known you for years, Kris, and you are always around her."

Kristoff's eyes narrowed. "My name is Kristoff, not Kris. And besides, it's not like that, Hanz. My mother forces me to be around her. She told me that if I am not nice to her, her dirty Jew father will likely fire my mother. My mother needs the work. My father died and left us flat broke. This is our only means of income."

Adolf, a heavy-set boy with deep dimples, broke in. "So, where are you running off to then?"

"I was running to get a hammer to help break windows tonight."

"Oh really?" Adolf said. "Well, to be sure of your loyalties, you stay with us tonight. We are keeping you away from her."

Kristoff stared Adolf down, his eyes focused on Adolf's pupils. "There will be no questioning my loyalties after tonight, Adolf. You will see."

The group of four boys left together and headed down the darkened alleyway towards Gunter's house to secure tools, clubs, and any item that could help cause damage. Walking down the damp street, Kristoff feared for the Blumenfelds' safety. He had no way to warn them, no way to tell them to get out of the house. If he tried to do so, he would risk his cover, and all would be lost. He took some consolation in the fact that the orders given instructed the youth not to kill anyone, only to cause property damage. "They may have damage to the store, but at least they will be alive," he told himself.

"Hey, Kristoff, how about we start at the Blumenfeld's shop. With any luck that girl Lorelei will be there, and who knows? Maybe we can run her out of town," Gunter taunted.

The hour of assault arrived, and Kristoff recognized he was several miles away from Lorelei's father's store. Gunter nervously kept checking his watch as if stalling or waiting for someone to make the first move. A loud crash of glass broke the silence of the night. A store window shattered onto the cement sidewalk four stores down the street from them. The sound was like a pistol being fired to start a race. The street was immediately infested with all sorts of men and boys smashing in store windows, kicking in doors, and torching buildings. Horrific screams and thick black smoke filled the air as Jews were being forced from their homes and shops. Gunter, Hanz, and Adolf ran off together laughing, kicking in doors, and throwing stones through windows.

During the commotion, Kristoff was left behind. He knew he must try to warn the Blumenfelds of the impending danger heading their way. He ran as fast as his legs would carry him, smashing glass into shards under his boots as he thundered down the street. The neighborhood looked so different with all the damage, and it was difficult to recognize where he was with so many buildings burning and the streets filled with smoke.

At length he found himself racing down a familiar street. He soon located the Blumenfeld's store. However, the front door was now laying inside, ripped from its hinges by a forceful blow. The window panes had all been dashed into shards, and tailored business suits had been torn to shreds and strewn throughout the street. The inside of the store was pitch-black, the electricity being cut off at its source. Kristoff headed through the darkened shop calling out for the Blumenfelds and Lorelei. A faint whimper came from the distant corner of the store near the staircase. Making his way to the weak sound, Kristoff found Lorelei's mother Martha bloodied, her hair disheveled, and her blouse torn.

"They took my Alfred!" she screamed in terror. "The SS took my Alfred!"

"This can't be!" Kristoff said. "Lorelei? Where is Lorelei?"

Martha lowered her head. "I don't know. They struck me on the back of my head right after they took Alfred, and everything went dark. I don't know where she is. I don't know if they took her or perhaps worse. Kristoff, go find my baby girl!" Her panic-filled voice filled all of his senses.

Kristoff raced up the stairs of the shop, and he coughed as the smoke from the fire on the second story choked off his air supply.

"Lorelei!" he screamed out in desperation. "Lorelei, where are you?"

The room was deathly still, except for the crackling of the fire. His worst fears began to build up inside him, and his stomach felt sick. Suddenly, the hiding place he had sworn to keep secret so many years ago appeared in his mind. Darting toward the hideaway, he hastily located the loose wooden slats on the floor covering it. With some force, he quickly extracted them. Pressed against the water storage cans and boxes of dry food, he could make out Lorelei's shape under a blanket. Rushing to her side, Kristoff uncovered her face, placed his left smoke-stained cheek to her nose, and felt a shallow warm breath expelled from her nostrils. At once, he pulled her unconscious body out of her hiding place and tossed her over his right shoulder. With a new sense of energy and adrenaline, he raced down the stairs, carrying her and leading Martha to the safety of the street.

Orange and red lights reflected from the street surface like starlight reflects on puddles after a recent rainstorm, though the street was dry. He proceeded cautiously with Lorelei balancing her on his weakening shoulder. Just a few steps onto the street, it became apparent to him that water did not reflect the light on the street; it was thousands of glass shards. They littered the street, bouncing back the light from the fires from the surrounding burning buildings.

Large jagged glass from the broken storefront windows blanketed the street. With each gentle step, Kristoff could hear the cracking and popping of glass as the weight of his heavy footsteps would crush the fragments under his boots. Martha's voice caught in her throat as she lamented, "This is truly a night of broken glass and dreams."

Kristoff scanned the road's surface for a section of cobblestone void of broken glass. His eyes narrowed, straining to find an area suitable to lay down Lorelei's motionless body. Spotting an area near the street corner, he made his way across the street with Martha following behind him.

Stepping over the street curb, he rested Lorelei on the sidewalk in front of him. "Lorelei, wake up. Lorelei, you're safe now. Breathe! I tell you, breathe! I plead with you Lorelei, wake up. I need you."

Her body was lifeless and still. Kristoff leaned over and whispered in her right ear. In this position, Kristoff could see Martha out of the corner of his eye rocking on her feet and rubbing her hands nervously, not knowing what to do for her unresponsive daughter. He gently grasped Lorelei's delicate hand. Kristoff closed his eyes, clearing his mind.

"Lorelei," he spoke softly, "I promise and pledge my life to protect you, your family, and all those that are being persecuted. I will not stop until this evil has been vanquished."

Her body remained motionless. He continued even softer. "Lorelei, I love you." He gently kissed her cheek goodbye and began slowly to stand up, staring down at her body, the reality of the grim situation painfully piercing his soul.

Perhaps it may never be known if she heard his words that he whispered in her ear or if it was divine intervention, but something miraculous happened. A tear slipped from the corner of her left eye, washing away ash in a thin streak as it trickled down her cheek. A raspy cough sputtered out of her lungs followed by a deep gasping breath of fresh air filling her chest. Her eyes cracked open.

Kristoff dropped back to his knees as she raised her right hand pressing the palm to Kristoff's flushed sweaty face. His lips widened into a smile, bearing testimony to Martha that her daughter was alive.

Martha stared as if she had seen a ghost. "Let it be known this day that a miracle happened on this night of broken glass," Martha proclaimed. "Come, let us be quick to leave. I fear that this day of violence is just the beginning of increasing terror. They will probably return with more numbers."

Lorelei sat up slowly. "But where can we go? Our shop was destroyed, and I saw them take father before I hid myself in the attic. What are we to do, Mother? Where are we to go?" Lorelei asked.

"This isn't the place to discuss this," Martha insisted, helping Lorelei to her feet and brushing small glass pieces from off her dress. "Kristoff, we must take refuge with you and your mother, Elsa, for the remainder of the night. We can discuss our options in the safety of your house."

The three agreed to the plan, turned, and quickly headed in the direction of Kristoff's home. Martha looked back over her shoulder one last time at the store where she had sacrificed so much to raise her small family.

7

Kettenkrad

Several weeks passed before Lorelei recovered from the events that transpired on the night of broken glass. Both Martha and Elsa took turns caring for Lorelei during that time, and they formed a tight friendship through the acts of service on behalf of Lorelei. With the formation of friendship, they discovered that they had many things in common. Through unfortunate events, both women had tragically lost a husband; however, Martha held out hope that she would be reunited with her dear Alfred once again.

Kristoff continued to be active in the Hitlerjugend and attended his meetings, training, and military exercises. He was extremely careful not to divulge his secret situation or blow his cover. During the evening dinners at home, he would repeat things that he had heard during the day regarding advancing military objectives and the ongoing persecutions of the Jewish people. He also reported the names of their friends and families they had known that had been hauled away to camps.

"It's terrible. They take everything from the Jewish people. All they have worked for, all that they saved. Everything has been taken from them. Paintings, furniture, everything. Nothing spared. Many books are being burned in nightly fires on the streets." The room fell mute as he described the horror in detail.

One night, Kristoff reported that homes would be entered by military force and any Jewish people refusing to leave would be sent to camps already prepared. The leaders had also stated that all homes would be searched, even those of military personnel, in order to ensure all Jews were moved out of the area.

"Elsa, Lorelei and I must leave at once!" Martha cried out. "If it is found out that we are kept here with you, both you and Kristoff will be harmed, or even worse."

Elsa closed her eyes to concentrate and quickly formulated a plan. "Martha, you and Lorelei can stay in the abandoned cottage at the edge of town. The house is in great disrepair. No one will suspect it to be occupied given its condition. The owner of that house passed away about ten years ago, and not a soul has entered it since that day. It will serve as a great hiding place until something more suitable can be acquired. I will provide food and supplies to the two of you during the night. You'll need to keep low, only use candlelight at night if necessary. You must board up any windows to prevent anyone from seeing the light. Hopefully, this will only be a few short weeks until we can better manage the ongoing situation."

Martha bowed her head in slight defeat. She fully understood the gravity of the circumstances and had succumbed to the bleak realization that it was the only option she had.

"Come, let us prepare some food, clothing, and blankets," Elsa insisted.

"Think of it as camping for a few weeks, Lorelei." Martha's voice trailed off as she reached under her bed to grab a wooden crate to help carry provisions.

The evening hours grew late while the women packed up the necessary items to sustain them for the next three or four days. They were limited to what they could carry in satchels as well as in the wooden crate.

Martha was careful not to pack too heavy because she needed to walk swiftly to their destination in the middle of the night.

"Mother, will this truly be enough for us?" Lorelei asked, looking concerned.

Martha grimaced. "It's sufficient for our needs. After all, Elsa will come by in a few days to provide us with more rations."

Martha wrapped a warm loaf of bread with a soft checkered cloth and placed it gently in the wooden crate. "Come, Lorelei, no further questions. The hour has arrived, and we must depart. Quickly, grab your belongings. The roads will be empty of travelers at this time of night, and we will not be seen. Come, let us not toil any longer."

It was clear to Lorelei that her mother didn't want to discuss the dire situation they were about to enter.

The women gathered up what they could carry and headed to the main door. Martha peeked her head out the door and inspected the roadway. "The road is clear," she whispered to Lorelei and Elsa.

Kristoff leaned forward in a wooden rocking chair, staring down the hall at his best friend. He prolonged the moment as long as he could, hoping that this moment would not actually arrive. So many thoughts had passed through his mind as he sat rocking forward and backwards for the past forty-five minutes. After racking his brain for a better solution, the only one that could be reached was the one that his mother had previously designed. It was true, they needed to conceal themselves from hateful Nazi soldiers. The situation at hand had now escalated to a level of extreme fear, something none of them had ever felt before. The German government, its laws, and leadership changed so quickly in what appeared to be almost overnight. New enforced laws and anti-Semitic preaching now tarnished the country they once loved and called home.

Kristoff walked slowly to the front door to where the women were standing. His face revealed his internal torment and crushing feeling inside his gut.

"Lorelei, Martha, do be careful. Know I am looking out for you, and I'll do everything and give everything, including my own life to protect you. I'll keep you informed as much as possible and try to lead away storm troopers from that rickety house."

Elsa sniffled and then quickly swiped at a tear with her dirty sleeve. "Go you two, go!" Elsa insisted.

Kristoff looked over at Lorelei and winked his left eye. Lorelei's quivering lips relaxed and stretched into a broken smile. The winking of the left eye was a long-established secret code the two of them came up with to tell one another, I love you. Lorelei squared her shoulders, looked back at Kristoff, and slowly closed her left eye into a soft wink. As quick as the wink, she stepped out the front door and was gone from his sight.

Kristoff's guts turned inside him and left him feeling that he had just abandoned his best friend. "It's the only solution, Kristoff," he murmured under his breath.

Martha's longer legs outpaced Lorelei's, and the haste of their march spurred Lorelei's calves to burn with every new step.

"Mother, we must slow down a bit. My legs blaze with fire. I can't keep up at this pace."

Martha looked back at her daughter. "So sorry. I'm just scared for our safety and want to get off this road as quickly as possible. You're right. We should slow ourselves down a bit."

Lorelei scrunched her face in deep thought. "Do you think we will ever see them again? After all, we haven't seen Father in several weeks and not a word of where he is has reached us."

Martha stopped, lowered the wooden crate to the ground, and stared directly into Lorelei's eyes. "Look, we don't know of your father's whereabouts nor of his current situation. We don't know how things will be tomorrow, in two days, or even next week. All we can do is be positive in our attitude and hope for the best. If we don't have hope, we have nothing at all. Personally, I find it best to say, 'I hope that we will see Kristoff and Elsa again.'"

Lorelei bent over and picked up the crate for her mom. "Mother, I'm sorry, I shouldn't have doubted, I only …."

"Shhhh," Martha said. "Not another word."

"But, Mother, I said I was sorry."

"No, I'm serious. Silence yourself. I hear something!"

The two held completely still, straining to hear every sound. Martha had not been mistaken. There was a low rumble of a noise being carried on the night's breeze.

"Quick, Lorelei, let's get off the road and hide in the bushes by the tree line."

The two raced to a line of tall trees and quickly hid the wood crate behind a large pile of old brush. Lorelei grabbed small branches, grass, and leaves to make a makeshift camouflage.

"Quick, Mother, lie down."

"Where did you learn how to do that?" Martha asked.

"Kristoff taught it to me. Something he learned in the Hitlerjugend. Stay low, Mother, and keep your head down no matter what. Don't let them see your face."

The rumbling sound intensified with every passing minute, and soon the ground they were lying on began to vibrate underneath them. Martha spotted a single faint yellow headlight in the distance heading their direction. It seemed to be the source of the peculiar noise.

Both women lay completely still and did not dare move a muscle. Lorelei tried to hide her fear behind tightly closed eyes. The unmistakable squeaking of metal tank tracks slapping on the road's surface could be clearly distinguished as the dim headlight approached the hiding place. The clatter of the tracks came to an abrupt stop on the road, and the humming of the motor idling made Lorelei's heart accelerate.

Cracking open her eyes, she could make out a small tank-like vehicle with the front end that resembled a motorcycle. Two Nazi soldiers wearing metal helmets could be seen in the dim light shining down from the overhead crescent moon. The man sitting on the back of the tank section angrily shouted at the driver, "Why are we stopped?"

The driver let go of the handlebars, climbed over the side of the vehicle, and stepped onto the dirt road.

"I need to relieve myself," he responded.

"Make it fast!" demanded the man, clearly in a position of leadership. "I want to finish this assignment and get back to the warmth of my bed. It is late and I have better things to do than patrol dirt roads at night in Kettenkrad."

The driver stepped away from the Kettenkrad and headed in the direction to where Martha was concealed. Martha's heart leaped out of her chest when she spotted her silk scarf lying on the ground in front of her. In the haste of hiding herself, she did not realize that the scarf she had tied around her neck had loosened and was now resting on the moist soil just an arm's reach away from her. *The Nazi soldier approaching me will discover this, and we'll be doomed*, she thought.

At that very moment, it was as if her hand had a mind of its own. Before she had time to think, her hand had launched forward, grasped the soft cloth in her trembling fingers, and proceeded to draw it back to her. Suddenly, her hand was pinned to the ground by a crushing force pressing downward. The dark of the night had kept her arm out of sight from the soldier's view; however, her speed had not been quick enough on retraction, and the Nazi soldier had stopped right on top of her hand, unaware that the heel of his long black boot was crushing it.

Martha's hand burned with pain as the soldier shifted his weight from foot to foot. It seemed like the bones in her hand were breaking under the pressure of the boot. The pain was excruciating. No sound escaped her mouth. Tears streamed down her dirty face as she suffered in silence. All Martha could do was clench her teeth tightly to keep from screaming.

The heavily uniformed German soldier finished relieving himself, took several steps backwards, which released Martha's pinned hand, then headed back to the Kettenkrad, completely unaware that he had just crushed a human hand. Martha refused to move while she listened intently to make sure the footsteps of the man headed in the opposite direction of her hiding place. Lying motionless, she could hear the rumble of the Kettenkrad motor increase with intensity once again. With the clatter of tank tracks fading in the distance, the men were gone as quickly as they had arrived. She finally let out a painful whimper, breaking the silence of the night as fresh wet tears tumbled down Martha's face.

Lorelei climbed out of the bushes and began removing the twigs and branches from her clothing and hair, piece by piece. "That was a close one, Mother. I thought we were done for. They were so close to us, it was disgusting. I could hear that man urinating," she said in a jovial tone. It was at this moment that Lorelei first noticed something was wrong with her mother.

Martha looked up at Lorelei. "I think my hand may be broken." Martha's face grimaced as she attempted to make a fist with her right hand. "Lorelei, gently hand me our box of provisions and let's be on our way."

Lorelei's eyebrows raised as she stared down at her mother's swollen hand. "Mother, how are you going to make the long walk carrying the loaded crate with your broken hand?"

Martha looked down at her throbbing hand. "The same way I did not scream as my hand was being crushed by that soldier's boot. I just push through the pain, Lorelei. Sometimes we just have to do hard things."

The two of them gathered their things once again and headed back to the vacant road. Resuming their journey Martha could feel her hand pulsating with pain and the size of her left hand was noticeably larger than before. The trauma sustained resulted with her only being able to move the first three fingers of her right hand with nauseating pain. During the remainder of the pilgrimage, Martha stopped every ten minutes or so to place down the wooden crate and rest. She took the same scarf that got her in this mess and wrapped her tender hand tightly with it, hoping to stabilize the hand.

At length, and with many stops along the way, the two of them arrived at the abandoned cottage. An uneasy feeling of loneliness enveloped the dwelling and the surrounding overgrown trees on the property. This uninvited feeling reminded Lorelei of the time Kristoff dared her to visit the local cemetery with him late at night to tell ghost stories.

Martha struggled to make the last few long steps to the house. The severe pain in her hand was now more than she could tolerate, and the moment to stop and rest for the remainder of the night was only a few more feet away. Stepping onto the front porch, the wood boards creaked under the weight of their fatigued feet as the two exhausted women approached the door. Setting their provisions down, Martha felt another sharp pain in her hand during the movement. This time Lorelei heard a small painful grunt come from her mother.

The front door had been left partially open revealing a large Nazi swastika marked in paint on the dry weathered wooden door. Glossy black paint dribbled down from the freshly painted swastika leaving streaks of wet paint that nearly reached the threshold. "Mother, don't go in!" Lorelei blurted out. "I believe those Nazi soldiers may have painted this on the door. They may still be inside."

The thought of Nazi soldiers searching inside this old building for anyone Jewish made Martha's stomach drop in protest. She took a deep slow breath filling her lungs to capacity and held her breath tightly. Attempting to calm her nerves and exhaling slowly, she motioned for Lorelei to crouch down on the wood porch just below the view of the window. Martha held completely still and listened intently for any movement inside the building. The stench of diesel fuel exhaust was hanging in the cool night air and the pungent smell burned inside her nostrils. Martha could hear her thundering heart inside her chest making it difficult for investigative listening, which further led to a dramatic increase in her anxiety. After several minutes of straining their ears for sounds within the house, Martha noted that the heavy smell of diesel fuel in the air had diminished significantly, purified by the gentle breeze.

"Lorelei, I'm going in to check inside the house. You stay right where you are." Martha crouched low and held her broken hand close to her body in an attempt to stabilize the injury and minimize the pain. *The soldiers must have departed from here moments before we arrived*, Martha hypothesized. Trusting her instincts, Martha pushed the door open slowly with her uninjured hand.

The limited moonlight breaking through the window revealed an empty entry way and a turned over table next to the kitchen. The old home looked quite abandoned with years of dust layered thickly on the interior fixtures and broken furniture. Two sets of boot prints disrupted the years of dust on the floor, leaving a trail where the soldiers had walked just moments before. It was evident that the Nazis entered the home, took a few steps around as they examined the abandoned building, and then marked the door with the swastika on their way out. The house was indeed clear, and her instincts had proven to be correct. Martha stood up, leaned back against the door, and let out a sigh of relief.

"Lorelei, it's safe, my dear. Come now, gather the provisions and let's go inside." The two fatigued women shuffled into the home, turned around, and secured the front door.

Lorelei retrieved a thin long candle from the wooden crate that she had hauled into the house. Striking a small wooden match, she pressed the flame to the candle wick. A soft flickering glow bounced back at them dancing off the barren, gray-wood walls. A sulfuric puff of smoke slowly dissipated from the tip of the match, illuminating Lorelei's eyes fixed intently on the burnt end. "What are you thinking about?" Her concern was evident in her pale face as she tried to arouse a response from her mesmerized daughter.

"Um, what?" she breathed out. The question was enough to break her intense stare and snap her back into reality.

Lorelei couldn't wrap her head around what was happening to her. Everything she once had known was now different. She no longer had a safe home, her father was hauled away, and Nazi soldiers hated her for her religion. The only thing that had kept her going was her deep love for Kristoff, and now she was taken away from him. Her stomach twisted and turned inside her like a washing machine off balance and the reality of it all hit her like a fist in the gut. She had been staring at the burning match and drifted off in her thoughts, hoping it was a bad dream from which she would suddenly awake.

Martha gently placed her arm around her daughter. "Come dear, let's rest for the night." Holding the dim light in front of them, the two tiptoed their way to the back room and fashioned a crude bed of blankets on the floor. Lying down, their heavy eyelids slammed shut the moment their heads hit the makeshift pillows made from rolled up clothing.

8

The Plan of Attack

Elsa stood in the kitchen of her home. She packed another basket loaded with jellies, breads, and leftover baked chicken from the night before. Almost a year had passed since her friends slipped away into hiding. Elsa knew that Martha had struggled physically for several months, relying completely on Lorelei for most of the tasks around the modest hideout. Having a hand injury made it difficult to provide assistance to her daughter. It didn't take long for the pair to discover that they should sleep during the day and work repairing the house at night in order to remain undetected. Within a few nights after arrival, the windows of the house were boarded up, masking out any movement inside the house that could be seen from plain view. For anyone passing by the house, it appeared to be abandoned and neglected. The swastika on the front door helped to complete the look and ensured that any passing Nazi patrol knew it had been previously inspected. The interior of the house was functional and served as a basic shelter. Minimal provisions continued to be smuggled in by Elsa late in the night and sometimes as often as twice a week.

During that year, Nazi-controlled Germany increased military raids on innocent Jews and forced many into holding camps guarded by men in towers with rifles and spotlights. Hitler had an agenda, and Poland was dead center in the crosshairs. Occupation of Poland was important to him, and he wouldn't stop until he possessed it. Rumors of the German Führer requesting secret meetings with the Soviet Union swirled around the Hitlerjugend meetings. It was speculated among the young militants that some cojoined effort with the Soviet Union to help take control of Poland. The boys in the Hitlerjugend believed that the plan would be presented and explained at an upcoming private military briefing that had been scheduled to take place at the end of August.

War was looming and the increased security around Germany prevented Kristoff from safe visits undetected with Martha and Lorelei. During the time apart, Kristoff only made two visits late in the night when his mother was unable to go for herself. His safety could not be jeopardized. If discovered, Kristoff would likely be executed. He was willing to take the risk. The mere thought of the anticipated visits with Lorelei made butterflies fly violently in his stomach bouncing off his ribcage in every direction. Though the visit was short, Kristoff cherished every second of it and his heart would sink like a submarine to the ocean floor the moment he was forced to return home.

The long time locked away weighed heavy on the women. Lorelei was developing cabin fever and dreamed of her freedom walking with Kristoff by the creek as she had done so often in the past. She imagined it so well, she often thought she could actually feel sunbeams warming her face as she pictured her and Kristoff lying in the soft grass along the side of the creek.

Kristoff did his best to share with them news sent though his mother describing the changes taking place around Germany. Both Germany and Poland were at the brink of war. Hitler's army continued to grow in strength, and little resistance was felt by the Nazi army's advancements. German victories were becoming common place and the advancing

Nazi armies pressed forward dominating every military engagement. Poland was well aware that its military paled in comparison to the modern Nazi engineering marvels, and was hoping for diplomatic resolutions, though an eventual battle was looming in the air.

Kristoff found himself home less frequently with the countless military details on a daily basis. The dark hate of Jews continued to escalate among the Hitlerjugend as planned by the Führer. This was ensured by his continual barrage of orders to inflict discomfort on the Jews, especially those from Poland. Most youth activities included the harassment of Jews in the streets as well as anyone showing sympathy for Poland. The youth had a constant bombardment of Nazi ideology, preaching of racism, and the belief that Germany must live, even if they, the youth, had to die for the pride and success of Germany. For these future soldiers, there was no escaping the entanglement of negative news that held them tightly. The constant hammering of indoctrination to ensure young Nazi loyalty was enforced by all military leaders under direct orders from Hitler himself. The limitless political goals of Hitler's totalitarian dictatorship were overflowing in classrooms like a lava bursting from a violent volcano.

Kristoff arrived early to the class today hoping to reinforce his facade of being an extremely loyal Hitlerjugend soldier. He spent the morning making sure his uniform was in tiptop shape. His black boots reflected a recent careful buffing job that one might mistake for an ebony mirror attached to the end of his feet. His tan long-sleeved shirt was wrinkle free and complemented the black knee-high shorts his mother had carefully pressed the night before. A long rolled black neckerchief was secured with a woggle, and Kristoff even went as far as polishing his chrome belt buckle. On his left sleeve, a red-white-red striped flag with a black swastika on top of a white diamond background completed the look. He was clean, well groomed, and looked like that of a military officer posing for a portrait.

His untimely arrival that morning interrupted a small group of boys huddled in a semicircle gossiping at the front of the class. From the back of the room Kristoff couldn't help but notice the new posters of Adolf Hitler displayed like royalty and draped on both sides of the chalkboard. Not wasting any time, he spotted his assigned desk on the fourth row and eased his way to his seat. Avoiding any eye contact with the group of boys, he sat at his desk, fidgeting with the dry skin on his fingers.

Straining his ears, he recognized Gunter trying to deepen his voice in order to sound older than he was and trying to control the conversation. *Who was he kidding? What a lie. It was apparent that this was not the normal voice of a teenage boy.*

A mixture of a young prepubescent voice with a deep vocal strain filled the room the instant Kristoff sat down at his desk. By all accounts the theatrics had worked. Gunter, the slim, freckled-nose boy did, in fact, command all the attention of the onlookers and wanted Kristoff to overhear his rhetoric.

"Boys, as you know, Hanz is privy to confidential matters that he overhears by listening behind his father's closed-door meetings."

Hanz was a neighborhood bully from an early age, and no doubt inherited his father's disrespect for anyone who wasn't true to the Führer. He mimicked his father's S.S. antics by tripping, kicking, or harassing the Polish and Jewish children in the streets. Most neighborhood children dreaded Hanz and found themselves ducking behind corners when they caught a glimpse of his greasy strawberry hair approaching. He was feared by all the kids, that is, all but Gunter and Kristoff.

For some unknown reason, Hanz was loyal to Gunter, even though Gunter was younger and smaller. It was believed that Gunter knew something about Hanz, something that he didn't want revealed to others. A secret so private, he was willing to do anything to keep it quiet, even let Gunter rule the group of boys. The knowledge that Gunter knew Hanz's deepest secret kept Hanz submissive to his younger violent counterpart.

"I overheard my father discussing secret plans of an invasion of Poland to take place September 1," Hanz said. "He was speaking to some high-ranking officers in his office one morning. We don't know who they were, only that they looked important. They wore long black boots and had on a uniform full of metals and ribbons."

"Get on with it already, Hanz!" said Adolf.

"Fine. As I was saying, there is some sort of German-Soviet pact that is to take place real soon that will partition Poland between the Soviet Union and Germany. Can't you see? This will enable us to attack Poland easily without any protection from the Soviets."

Adolf butted in once again. "So, what's the plan of attack?"

Gunter tilted his head slightly to the right and squinted his eyes.

"The details were hard to hear, Adolf," he said, his voice trailing off. "I do remember hearing something about thousands of tanks and planes that will be used in a surprise attack. These forces are certain to break through the outdated Polish defenses, and we will encircle Warsaw. From what I could make out, the Soviet Union will help ensure our success."

Gunter's smile suddenly stretched from ear to ear, exposing his crooked yellowing teeth. He obviously wanted in on the action, and the thought of war pleased him to his rotten core. "This is great, boys," he said. "Maybe we can start eradicating all Jews." Gunter flashed a devious look in Kristoff's direction and raised his voice. "We can even get rid of that ugly dog you used to be seen with, Kristoff. What was that mutt's name again?"

A few boys in the circle chuckled.

Kristoff's blood was boiling to the point of eruption. He had been pretending that he could not hear the group and was thumbing through paperwork at his desk. The insult about his best friend (and girlfriend) had taken all the strength he could muster not to lash out at Gunter.

A wave of fury flushed across his face just as the dry brass hinges supporting the classroom door unexpectedly let out a piercing squeak that protested the weight of the swinging heavy wood. The shrill emanating from the hinges startled the secretive circle of cadets, who suddenly clammed up the moment the instructor walked in the room. Gunter's band of followers took their seats at the front of the room. Gunter also sat down and slowly looked back over his right shoulder, making eye contact with Kristoff. The devilish smirk on his face bore testimony to Kristoff that he either suspected something or had information on Kristoff and Lorelei.

9

The Invasion

"I can't sleep," mumbled a frustrated voice from the top military bunk. Kristoff was consumed with the events that were about to be unleashed upon the unsuspecting Polish. "I wish I could somehow warn Poland of this impending attack." His thoughts bounced around inside his skull like a metal ball in a pinball machine. "But what can I possibly do? I have no way to help them. They are sitting ducks with hunters approaching on all sides of the pond," he grumbled out loud.

"Shut it, Christkindl! You're talking in your sleep again!" came the agitated voice of Gunter from the lower bunk. Evidently Gunter was not sleeping well either, though for much different reasons than Kristoff. Gunter was excited and even anxious to hunt the innocent unsuspecting victims. For certain, this boy was born without a conscience and did not value human life.

Days earlier under direct orders, Kristoff and the Hitlerjugend had been feverishly preparing for a surprise attack on Poland. Military fighter planes and bombers had been stuffed with ammunition, tanks had been armed for war, and were currently poised in position to stop any resistance. Many thousands of German troops had been made ready and sent to their strategic holding positions, waiting anxiously to pounce on the unsuspecting Polish citizens.

For young Kristoff, it was surreal, yet well-orchestrated. The menacing plan of attack had been sent in motion, and strategic maneuvers loomed, waiting for the precise time to advance. Several weeks earlier, Adolf Hitler concocted a cunning plan to make it appear that Poland had aggressively attacked a German border post unprovoked. Polish military uniforms were placed on dead bodies to help spawn the illusion of a small battle that had ensued, though completely initiated by Poland's forces. In his fraudulence, Hitler had created his justification for an attack on Poland.

Kristoff's racing thoughts were uncouthly interrupted in the middle of the night when the barrack overhead light beamed directly into his eyes coupled with a thunderous voice screaming at him to "arise and go to battle!" The commander's ear-splitting voice reverberated off the surrounding barrack walls, piercing the ear drums of the sleeping young men. The entire room was now in commotion with boys scrambling to get in their uniform.

It was the morning of September 1, 1939, and Germany was heading to war. Nazi forces moved around with eagerness anticipating a quick victory over Poland. Kristoff finished lacing his boots and secured them tightly. Reaching over to his footlocker, he grabbed his hat and headed outside to line up in military formation. Kristoff was considered a loner and somewhat of an outsider among his Hitlerjugend peers, mostly because of his stark ideological beliefs. He often found it best not to associate with the other boys and avoided any conversations that may provide insight to his past or his close Jewish friendships. Being a faithful friend had an immense strain on him, leaving him secluded from others.

"Christkindl, get in line! Hurry up, stop making us wait!" barked his commander.

A snicker could be heard coming from the direction where the proud Gunter was standing proudly.

Kristoff assembled himself in the back row of boys and stood firmly at attention. Standing among these boys, in Kristoff's mind, was being unfaithful to his true friends and his sweetheart, Lorelei. *I swear and promise to the heavens above that I will protect the inflicted Polish Jews on this mission, even if I must sacrifice my own life,* Kristoff pledged silently to himself.

Commander Auerswald stood confidently at the front of the formation of Hitlerjugend and studied them from left to right. He cleared his throat and began addressing the youth. "Around 4:30 this morning, more than one and a half million German troops will invade Poland all along our 1,700-mile border. The Luftwaffe will be bombing Polish airfields and our naval forces will be attacking the Polish Navy in the Baltic Sea. My dear young friends, this will bring Lebensraum, a great living space for the German people!" he shouted enthusiastically.

"Heil Hitler!" erupted from several of the boys standing with puffed chests. Kristoff remained silent.

"We have been commanded to enter the city after the attack to ensure no filth is left behind," the commander continued. "Special inescapable camps surrounded by razor wire and armed watchmen in towers have been made ready to hold them. Make sure to notify us if you encounter resistance from any Jews hiding like cowardly dogs. Nobody is excluded. All males, females, the old, or even the very young. If any try to attack, you have my personal permission to take whatever force you need to deescalate the situation. I promise you, my faithful Hitlerjugend, they will be dealt with swiftly and death will come to anyone wanting to resist Hitler or his forces." His dry, pursed lips stretched into a malicious grin, revealing several chipped, coffee-stained teeth.

Kristoff stood firm in military formation; his stony eyes fixed in the direction of the loud commander. He felt his teeth grinding under the pressure of his clenched jaw of defiance. He was on his own mission now. A mission to help liberate the oppressed.

Three weeks passed. The invasion had been a huge success for the German army, and they had advanced through Poland with little resistance against a less prepared Polish military. Many Polish had been forced into concentration camps or abandoned their homes and were now homeless.

The young men had been busy doing ongoing drills the morning of September 22 when Lieutenant Liebehenschel approached the Hitlerjugend.

"Gather your gear and load up, boys, you are heading to the war," barked his commander. Kristoff grabbed his gear as instructed and headed to a large idling military truck he was assigned to. Thick diesel exhaust filled his nostrils as he stood behind the truck to open the canvas flap. Flipping open the right flap, he was greeted by a pair of black boots at eye level and several faces peering down at him. "A hand stretched down from the inside of the truck's rear, offering assistance to climb on board. Kristoff tossed his pack inside and seized the outstretched arm. With one firm tug, Kristoff was hoisted up into the back and quickly sat down on the wooden bench.

Kristoff surveyed the area of young men wedged into the troop transport. Many faces with empty eyes peered down at the floor of the truck, refusing to make eye contact with anyone or risk sparking up a conversation. A slumped-over figure in the corner with boyish features could be seen massaging his eyes with his right thumb and index finger. Over and over in gentle slow semicircles, the boy continued rubbing his moist eyelids. The adolescent was not fooling anyone. They knew he wasn't suffering from seasonal allergies or ocular irritation from the exhaust of the diesel truck. No, he was actually doing that which all in his company wished they could do without harassment—shed a few tears.

Heads bobbed from right to left inside the transport as the truck bounced down the rugged back roads heading to Warsaw. The hypnotic rocking movements of their bodies magnified the ever-increasing fatigue, building up during the prolonged journey. A young freckled-face boy was completely unaware that he was resting his head on the shoulder of the boy to the right of him. Overwhelmed with sleep, the heavy-eyed boy made a makeshift bed out of a soft shoulder.

Someone tapped Kristoff's right shoulder. Turning his head in the direction, Kristoff locked eyes with the boy next to him. A short stocky boy with a stubby nose dotted with freckles stared at him with a cheesy grin. His slightly pointed ears stretched upward, drawing attention to his most notable feature, which was disproportionate compared to his peers, or even the general public, for that matter. The unique shape of his ears were undoubtedly likely the source of endless bullying and schoolyard fights. Unfortunately, the curious shape of his ears distracted from his kind, speckled, hazel eyes with moon-sized pupils.

"Hello, my name is Eckerd Lambart Fichtmann the Third." His right hand extended forward, requesting a formal greeting.

Kristoff returned the salutation. "Eckerd, that's your name?" A hint of uncertainty could be detected in his voice.

"Yes, Eckerd. My mom told me that the name actually means 'sacred.' It's kinda funny in a way." He chuckled.

Kristoff glanced up. "Why is it funny?"

"Well, I'm told that my last name means 'spruce tree,' so I guess I'm a sacred spruce tree."

The boys joined together in a good laugh, something Kristoff had not felt in quite some time. It felt good inside for Kristoff to laugh after so many months of darkness and not speaking or laughing with Lorelei.

"Well, Eckerd, it is nice to meet you. My name is Kristoff Nikolaus Christkindl."

The two boys let out another laugh.

"Well, that's a mouthful to say. Do you mind if I call you Kris for short?"

Kristoff shrugged his shoulders. "Sure, no problem. I haven't been called Kris in a long time. Go ahead, call me Kris."

Prior to this moment, only a few people had ever called Kristoff by his nickname: his father, Lorelei, and his mother. Being called Kris once again dragged his memory back to the last time he heard his father's voice.

"Be good, Kris. Take care of your mother while I am at work." His father picked him up, cradling him in his arms and squeezed him with a dad-tight loving hug. Kris wiggled his way out of the hug and back to the floor. This was a regular daily routine that he shared with his father that led his father to chase after him through the house in an understood game of tag.

"Not today, Kris. There has been a problem in the factory, and they need me right away," said his father, disappointed. Kristoff's father was a hard-working man, loyal, and always looked out for others, including at work. Bending down to Kristoff's level, he leaned over and kissed his forehead tenderly. Straightening up, he turned to Elsa and softly pressed his lips to her warm cheek.

"I'll see ya as soon as I get done." He grabbed his coat and work equipment off the wooden rocking chair by the front door, turned back to Kristoff, and winked his left eye. "We will play tag when I get back, Kris. Remember to take care of your mother." He pivoted on his heels and walked out the front door. It was the last time he would see his father alive. If he had known it would have been his last night with his father, Kristoff would have not wiggled out of the hug.

"Well, if I call you Kris, this must mean that we are now friends!"

The two boys exchanged laughs once again. They young men had been so engrossed in conversation, they did not even notice the movement of the truck had stopped, and that they had entered the war zone.

"Get out and huddle by the roadside just over there!" their commander yelled. He pointed toward the front of the line. "I'll give you instructions in a moment. Quickly now! Huddle up."

A small stampede of young men piled out of troop transports and rushed to the side of the road to await assignments. Eckerd and Kristoff stood next to one another, both happy to have a new friend, yet miserable to be standing on the roadside awaiting orders. The truck had stopped next to a bombed-out building left in rubble at the edge of town. Hanz and Gunter were standing close together, talking in hushed voices out of earshot from the rest of the group. "I can't believe they transferred Adolf to Berlin," whispered Hanz. "It's on account of him being overweight that made him unfit for combat so they had to send him to Berlin to do less strenuous things in a mailroom. I guess it's down to just the two of us now Hanz." Gunter sighed.

Clunking footsteps smacked the ground as the commander approached the huddled cadets.

"Achtung!" said a husky cadet to the left of Kristoff.

Simultaneously the group of boys straightened their backs, drawing their arms close to the body, squaring the shoulders. Every head was facing forward, eyes fixated on an unseen object in the distance. Not even a dog staring down its opponent in a potential duel could compare to the frozen look of the young men. "Kompanie, ruhrt euch!"

The young men widened their stance, now standing at ease.

"Loyal Hitlerjugend," said their new commander Wilhelm Schwarz. "You are to go in groups of two and sweep the city, removing valuables of any kind, including furniture. Enter every home, shop, or building, and flush out anyone hiding. We are to cleanse Poland so our German people can move in. Armed soldiers will be positioned in the streets and will force all prisoners onto awaiting trains that will haul them away. You'll need to check very carefully for anyone hiding out in the building you search. If you encounter any Jews, command them to leave. If they refuse, blow on your whistle and an armed soldier will come to assist you. If they continue to refuse to leave, they will be shot. Your task is essential, and our Führer has complete faith in your abilities. You are entering an area that has recently engaged in heavy fighting. Our fierce attack was extremely successful pushing the Polish army to the east during the past three weeks. You'll likely not encounter any fighting. Good luck, my dear young soldiers. Move out!"

Kristoff and Eckerd grouped up and began walking through the rubble of the war-ravaged city of Warsaw. Chunks of burnt red bricks were strewn across the street from the blast of enemy fire, making it impossible for motorized vehicles to pass. Bullet holes perforated the walls of the buildings surrounding the street, and battered vehicles remained in the exact location for the past three weeks since the invasion. Streetlamps were snapped in two like dry toothpicks, rubble from the bombed buildings covered sidewalks in mounds, and columns of dark smoke in the distance stretched high into the sky. Beautiful cathedrals had been leveled to piles of brick and mortar. All the destruction was difficult to take in, especially for Kristoff.

"Eckerd, what makes us better than them? Why are we inflicting pain and persecution on them for a religion?"

Eckerd looked at Kris. "This war doesn't make much sense to me either." Eckerd lowered his head and kicked a piece of broken brick out of his way.

The two young soldiers entered homes and looked for any occupants as commanded. After inspecting a dozen or so buildings, the young men had concluded that any remaining people had long abandoned the area. They continued with their orders, entering building after building, searching for anyone hiding out. Each new building created unique challenges. Each building had become entirely unstable and unsafe to enter, though the youth dare not question their commanding officers.

Paintings, furniture, and precious items left behind in a hasty exodus were gathered in large piles and enclosed in wooden crates bound for Germany. Eckerd was laying a large oil portrait of a sizable woman in a stack of artwork outside of a crumbling building when he heard a high-pitched whistle in the distance. Eckerd peered over the stack of priceless artwork and noted two young men marching behind a family.

"Hanz and Gunter found a family. Come look, Kris."

Hanz was pushing a young girl in the back, forcing her to walk faster. Gunter had a broken piece of wood in his hand and would tap it on the back of the legs of the man who was walking with his hand in the air.

"I want to slap the smile off Gunter's face," said Eckerd.

Kristoff glanced at Eckerd. *Could Eckerd share the same feelings about this war?* he thought. "Eckerd, let's just do our best to stop any others from being discovered. Come, let's continue to search."

Kristoff and Eckerd had reached a four-story building with a large arched doorway gracing the front entrance. The building was well preserved from the invasion and had somehow avoided the flurry of bullets and bombs. "This one looks like a good place to hide," Eckerd said, surveying the building. "Let's check it out."

The two strong boys forced their way into the building. The kitchen cabinets had been left open and the shelves were barren. The rooms were clean and orderly, various oil paintings still on nails hammered into the plaster-covered brick walls. A large rectangular-shaped dirt outline of a previously hung portrait in the entry room was visible from the front door. Years of hanging next to the fireplace had stained a soot outline around the family's most prized artwork. Someone clearly did not want to leave this particular picture behind.

Eckerd and Kristoff began their routine inspection of the home. Closets, cupboards, and even floorboards were inspected as commanded. By the time the boys had reached the fourth floor, the young men had removed from the home twelve miscellaneous paintings, numerous pieces of furniture of varying sizes, and considerable bundles of valuables.

"Kris, this was the last floor. Let's head out and go to the next building." Unexpectedly, the overhead wooden beams gave a low moan of protest. Catching Kristoff's attention, his eyes glanced upward in the nick of time to see dust particles slipping through the ceiling overhead and spilling onto the floor. Kristoff tapped Eckerd on his left shoulder and pointed up to the dust breaching through the cracks. With widened eyes and a jackhammering heart, Eckerd stared down Kristoff. "Someone is hiding upstairs, Kris."

10

Ageless Details

Kristoff sucked in air, swelling his chest to maximum capacity and stretched his rib cage to breaking point. Holding his breath, he could hear creaking boards above Eckerd's head, ten feet away from him. Another moan of dried wood was heard to the left of Kristoff, who was now letting his breath out slow and quietly.

"Someone is definitely moving around upstairs, and likely more than just one person. What should be done, Kris?" asked Eckerd.

Kristoff inhaled deeply once again and let out his breath gently, buying a little time to come up with a plan. "We know our commands, and we have been instructed what to do. Get your whistle ready in case we encounter trouble.

Eckerd turned his head, studying the ceiling. "How did they get up there? There must be a hidden door or entry," Eckerd whispered.

Simultaneously, the eager duo focused on the dusty weathered bookshelf in the far corner of the room.

"Let's check it out, Eckerd."

The boys approached the shelf and after a few minutes of inspection, grabbed the right side of the shelf, giving it a firm jerking tug. Without resistance, the shelf swung open freely on hidden hinges, exposing a shower-sized shaft with a wooden ladder ascending to the attic.

"That's it, Kris. Great work! We found it."

The dry hinges squealed in protest the moment the shelf was opened.

"I think they know we found the opening," observed Kris. "Let's not waste time. I'll go up the ladder first. You stand here at the ready to sound the alarm."

Kristoff grabbed the wooden rung, and in a flash scaled the ladder. Eckerd listened intently for a sign to sound the alarm. He could hear Kristoff pacing back and forth above him searching the area, small clouds of dust slipping down from above.

"Stand up and show your hands!" Kristoff's frightened command resonated down the shaft. "All of you stand up and head down the ladder. Listen closely, we're not going to hurt you and we don't want to cause a ruckus. My partner stands ready to sound the alarm, inviting armed soldiers to join us if any attempt to flee."

Kristoff motioned them with his hand to head towards the passage shaft. The lack of light in the hideout obscured the facial details of the family passing in front of him. As far as Kristoff could tell, there were three small children, one woman, and two men that descended into the room below.

The family lined up against the wall, all looking down at the floor. They refused to look up or make any eye contact.

"Are you Jewish?" asked Eckerd.

Nobody responded. Starting with the small children, Kristoff asked each one their name.

A small boy with a quivering chin responded first. "My name is Dieter. I'm seven."

Another boy said firmly, "Manfred. Ten."

A girl with a set of light brown eyes peered upward and squeaked out, "Ursula and I'm thirteen years old."

Kristoff stepped to the right and stood in front of the adults. "Please tell me your names so I can write them down."

"I'm Brigit, and this is my husband, Victor."

The man on the far right held silent.

Kristoff walked over and stood directly in front of him. "Sir, please, your name. I need your name."

The thick-bearded man raised his head slowly but did not look Kristoff in the eyes. His round glass spectacles were dirty and neglected. The left lens was cracked and spotted. The metal framed glasses had been previously bent and reshaped in a crude repair, likely the result of previous altercation.

"Your name, sir," Kristoff said again.

The man clenched his teeth and murmured his name.

"Once again, sir. I didn't quite get it."

The man's dim eyes peered through his foggy lenses.

"We are all of the Blumenfeld family. My name is Alfred, Alfred Blumenfeld."

Kristoff leaped back and began rubbing the back of his own neck while he processed what the man had just revealed.

Is it possible? Kristoff thought. "Lorelei!" The name spilled out of his mouth before he could stop it. The bearded man raised his head once again, squinting through his one good lens.

"My heavens! Kristoff is that you?"

Kristoff's legs weakened and he collapsed to his knees at the feet of Lorelei's father. Eckerd looked on, trying to process what was happening.

"Stand up, son. Let me look at you. You're so much taller than I remember. Look here, you're a Nazi soldier."

"Hitler Jugend!" said Kristoff aggressively.

The Blumenfeld children, Victor, and Brigit stared at the scene unfolding in front of them. Eckerd slowly walked over and put his arm around Kristoff. Leaning over, he whispered in his ear.

"Kris, it appears to me that you know this man. I can't think of a better time to start doing the right thing than at this very moment. Let's keep this family safe and not alert the soldiers in the street. We can simply mark the home as inspected and move on to the next building."

One thing was for certain, Kristoff had been an apparent good judge of character when he befriended Eckerd. It was clear that they did share the same feelings about the war and the treatment of the Jews.

"Everyone, back upstairs," commanded Kristoff. He stood up straight, clearly in charge. "If we're in this building much longer, the soldiers in the street will grow suspicious. Quickly now, back up the ladder and hide."

The family raced up the ladder and out of sight. Mr. Blumenfeld remained behind. "There is so much to tell you, Mr. Blumenfeld, but I don't want to risk exposing your hiding place. Lorelei and Martha are hiding in an abandoned cottage near my home. Mother is seeing to their safety and provisions. I have been in communication with them, though not in several weeks. All was good to that point. They miss you dearly and fear the worst. Many Jews are being captured and shipped out on trains like cattle. I understand they're heading to camps to work for the Führer. From what I have heard, if they don't want to work, they'll be executed. Martha and Lorelei never stopped believing you were alive."

Tears swelled up in Mr. Blumenfeld's eyes. One dribbled down his dingy cheek. "Kristoff, please get the word out to my family that I'm well and have taken refuge with my brother Victor in Warsaw after I broke free from captivity. It's a miracle I survived. I wish I could say the same about the men that tried to flee with me. Listen, we will hold up for a few more days before we will try to make our way to the Warsaw Zoo. My brother Victor has information that the Danes are secretly sending their Jewish countrymen to Sweden by means of dangerous boat crossings. We hope to join them. I've been in danger of losing my life since the day I was taken from my family. With any luck, Martha and Lorelei can get here soon so we can all go together. Kristoff, stay true to your convictions and protect the innocent at all costs. May our God protect you." Alfred kissed Kristoff on the cheek and scurried up the rickety ladder and out of sight.

"Kristoff, let's head out of the building and move on to the next."

Kristoff looked back over his shoulder at the now closed bookshelf hiding the passage opening. His stomach clenched deep inside his gut. This may be the last time he may ever see Lorelei's father alive.

The two young men descended the stairs and out to the street. A Nazi storm trooper leaned against a wall on the corner of the street smoking a cigarette. The soldier looked over at the boys and gestured to them to continue searching the adjacent building. Eckerd raised his hand and signaled back to the soldier that he understood the order and together they jogged to the next building.

"I think we're good, Kristoff. That soldier doesn't suspect a thing. Let's go. We need to talk."

Kristoff spent the next several hours inspecting buildings and telling Eckerd of his past and of his desire to protect people against the Nazi party. Eckerd took this time to also admit his past: his mother was Jewish, though this was unknown to the German Nazi party. She was not active in her Jewish religion, and when persecutions started, if ever asked of her faith, she would begin praying and praising Christ in order to lead away any suspicions. This worked well. Having Eckerd join the Hitlerjugend ensured the palter.

Mr. Amesbury was so engrossed in the conversation with the man claiming to be Santa that he had lost all track of time. "That was the beginning of a long friendship with Eckerd that continues to this very day," Kristoff Christkindl reflected, leaning back in the overstuffed chair. His head was pressed against the cushioned seat and he stared poignantly at the ceiling.

"Look here," he said, a slight chuckle accompanying his words, "where did the night go? My apologies, Mr. Amesbury, I have rambled on long through the night." The first rays of sunlight pierced through the slits in the wooden blinds, lighting the room.

Mr. Amesbury glanced down at his watch and rubbed his eyes. *Six a.m., and I'm not even tired, though a little hungry again.*

The skinny gray-haired man entered the room once again. "I hope I'm not intruding. I wondered if you would like a Danish and some juice?"

Kristoff glanced upward. "Your timing is impeccable. Thank you, Eckerd." A smile of appreciation stretched across his thin wrinkled face. Mr. Amesbury watched as the bull-legged man turned and walked away.

"Eckerd, did you say? That was Eckerd?"

Mr. Christkindl did not respond to Mr. Amesbury's question. He stood up from his overstuffed chair, pushing it backward out of the way and gave a good needed stretch to his legs.

Walking to the window, he opened the blinds, allowing additional sunlight to fill the room, which revealed several framed pictures and an oil painting. It showed small children gathered around a woman holding a basket of oranges. Many of the smiling children were reaching upward requesting a handout; one child was eating an orange alone with his back to the circle of children.

In the foreground of the painting, a little girl with golden hair and a blue summer dress was placing a slice of orange in a young boy's mouth. The woman in the painting was wearing a dark dress that complemented her slim figure, warm cheeks accentuating her heart shaped face and dark flowing hair peeked out from under her scarlet scarf. The woman stared down caringly at the children. A tear-stained cheek captured the attention of all who peered at the canvas by a skilled artist's hand.

"Oh, how I adore that painting you are staring at, Mr. Amesbury." Mr. Christkindl left the window and approached the large gold-framed painting hanging on the wall. Tapping on the basket of oranges in the painting with his thick index finger, he asked, "Joseph, do you know what the oranges in this painting represent?"

The reporter paused, interlocked his fingers in front of him on his lap, and contemplated the question. After a brief moment, Joseph said, "Well, I suppose it is nutrition, sweetness, something desirable."

"Oh, this is true. Yes, yes, Joseph, it is all of those things, and even more. It is as you said nutrition, and that provides life. Sweetness of the orange brings happiness, and something desirable, yes indeed. Just as in life, Joseph, there are things in this world that make us smile, provide happiness, and have essential life-sustaining abilities. This painting is not about an orange, it is so much more. Friends, family, belief that life has a higher purpose, selflessness, service, love, charity, kindness, Christlike attributes. This is what I see in the painting. Look closer at the children, Mr. Amesbury. So, can you determine their attitudes in the painting?

Joseph studied the painting closer. "I see children reaching up for the desire to be happy, a child selfishly consuming the orange in secrecy, and a caring girl sharing her one and only orange with another child, possibly a stranger."

"Now you're beginning to see more clearly about the real meaning of life. It's not about money, things of the world, and the constant quest to be better than your neighbor. Life is about doing what our Maker would do if he were here with us: provide life, happiness, and unselfish service."

The room fell silent and warm as the two men studied the painting. "Yes, that was Eckerd," Mr. Christkindl said abruptly.

"I beg your pardon, what was that?" Joseph flashed a questioning look toward the white-bearded man.

"I was answering your last question, you see. Yes, that was the same Eckerd I have known for so many years. What a dear friend."

"But the two of you look to be in your early sixties, not your mid-nineties, as the math would add up to be."

Mr. Christkindl stroked his thick white beard slowly with his left hand, occasionally rolling his mustache between his fingers.

"You are too kind, Mr. Amesbury. Why, just the other day I thought I saw a new gray hair." The chubby man chuckled, brushing his wavy white hair back with his hand. "Joseph, you're quick to the small details of a developing story. I knew I was right to choose you to reveal my story. You're correct, in a way. Yes, I look like I'm in my sixties, but as you know, looks can be deceiving. Joseph, your journey here tonight to sit with me was surrounded by unexplainable events. From the time you followed the Schnauzer on the street, to the animated frosted windowpane at the front door, the magic is all real, Joseph. That same magical force that led you here tonight is found coursing through my blood and makes up the very fibers woven together, prolonging my life on this earth. Yes, it is true, I do look about thirty years younger than I am. This mortal frame will always look this age. That is, given the image of Santa stays the same. You see, I take the form the people have created and imagined Santa to be like. This image, of course, comes from the hands of skilled artists and marketing specialists. White beard, soft warm red cheeks, and chubby as a loving grandfather. I often wonder what I would look like if people imagined a Santa that looked like a Roman God." His large stomach jiggled as he let out a laugh.

Joseph's smile widened, exposing his perfectly straight white teeth. It was becoming more apparent that Mr. Amesbury was feeling comfortable talking to Kristoff. "Now, I'm not saying I believe your story, Kristoff, but let's say that I do. How can you explain to me your existence before your birth in . . ." Joseph paused, looked downward, and began flipping through his notes, searching for a date he had jotted down early that night. "Ah, here it is. Yes, as I was saying . . . how can you explain your existence before your birth in 1925? It's obvious that you, or should I say, it's obvious that Santa folklore has been around long before 1925."

"I'm not the only Santa that has lived on this earth, Mr. Amesbury. No, actually there have been many of us, though only one can hold the supreme office of Santa at a given time. As a Santa Claus, we're called to this work at a time that was appointed to us while we're on the earth. Yes, there was another before me." His voice trailed off and he sucked in a long deep breath that expanded his ribcage to bursting point. Kristoff began twisting the ring on his right middle finger with his left thumb and index finger.

Joseph couldn't help but notice the ring. It was a brilliant gold with unusual writings and curious shapes of all different sizes engraved into the precious metal, though Joseph could not make out any familiar text. Alternating rubies and emeralds in a linear fashion circled the band with a feeling of royalty. One ruby was missing, leaving a space between the precious gems.

Kristoff stopped fiddling with his ring and continued, "Yes, before me was a great man we knew as Santa. I try my best to be like him. After all, it was he that saved me and called me to this work."

"I'm a little short on the details, Mr. Christkindl. Can you enlighten me?"

Kristoff turned away from Joseph and returned to his armchair, where he resumed sitting. "You want more details, do you? The details are all around you, Joseph. The details all have a story, and a story is what I promised to give you. Come with me, Joseph, back to the war, back to the Third Reich."

11

Lorelei's Last Words

"The year was now 1943 and I was no longer involved in the military as a Hitlerjugend. I was now fully involved as a Nazi military soldier. Uncomfortable in my own uniform, I felt like an ink drop on a mound of snow. I just didn't belong with them. I was very much opposed to treating anyone in this manner and refused to be indoctrinated by the madness. I lived with the hopes of being able to liberate the Jewish people under attack while dressed in Nazi robes. I had only joined the Hitlerjugend in order to protect Lorelei, her family, and anyone else I could. I never could have imagined that leaders of a country would go as far as rounding up faithful religious people, many of which were being murdered.

"We are all the same, Joseph! Please don't you ever forget this. What I am trying to say is that we are all part of the human race. We may not all be from the same county, backgrounds, or religious beliefs, but we all have been created by the same God, even though he may be called by a different name. We all share the same God, and this God is our Father making us on earth all brothers and sisters. Think about it: those men and women who were oppressed in the war, they were truly our

84

brothers and sisters.

"Joseph, I was an only child and I always wanted siblings. I tried to look at those around me as my family. This was difficult at times, I do admit, especially around Gunter or others who were filled with anger and hate. The war up to this point had intensified and the German army continued sweeping their invasions across Europe, enslaving and murdering the Jews along the way."

Joseph looked down at his pile of notes on his lap, looking at his last written note. "So, in your story earlier, you never finished telling me about what happened to Alfred Blumenfeld?"

"Well, it must have been a dirty, stinky escape," the chubby man said, chuckling. "It was amazing and almost hard to believe, but Mr. Blumenfeld, the Jewish suit maker, did accomplish his plan of escape from that building to the Warsaw Zoo—through the sewer system! He joined other Jews hiding for safety."

"What about Martha and Lorelei? Did they get reunited with Alfred?" Joseph's second question came quicker than his first.

"Now, this is where things really changed for me when it comes to the war, Joseph. The events that followed after Warsaw is what led me to become who I am today. I know you must be eager to know how it happened. Let me take you step by step. First off, I eventually reunited with my mother to let her know about Alfred and his plan. I instructed her to get word to Lorelei and Martha so they could make their way to the Warsaw Zoo. My mother was successful getting the word to Martha and Lorelei, and they left their hideout to Warsaw.

"Unfortunately, upon approaching Warsaw, they were discovered by a patrolling Nazi soldier, who attempted to arrest them. When confronted by the soldier, both Martha and Lorelei took off running in opposite directions. Quickly separating from one another was a good instinct because it made it difficult for an arrest and caught the soldier off guard, so he never had time to use his weapon. The arresting soldier pursued Lorelei, which allowed Martha time to hide.

"Sadly, both Lorelei and the soldier were not seen again by Martha. For three days, Martha hid under a canopy of shrubbery, and during the night she would search for Lorelei. Unsuccessful in locating her daughter, Martha feared for the worse and abandoned her search. I can only imagine how difficult of a decision this was. After all hope was lost, she pressed on to Warsaw, grieving. The poor woman was tired, out of food, and was forced to drink water from muddy puddles or water along the roadside. It was a miracle she survived her journey, but eventually Martha did arrive in Warsaw.

"Entering the city, several men hiding from patrolling German soldiers noticed her and quickly got her out of sight. She spent several days recovering with this caring group of men, and eventually shared with them of the hardship of losing her daughter and her rigorous venture. In time, a genuine trust developed among the new group of friends, and she entrusted them with her plans to get to the zoo. The men were familiar with Warsaw, and two of them had actually been through the tunnels years prior as curious exploring boys. To say the least, it did not take much convincing to get them onboard with her plan and after some difficulty navigating the tunnels, they led her through the sewers of the city to the zoo. I can only imagine the reunion with her husband, though I also imagine that the happiness was quickly suppressed by the unknown whereabouts of their missing daughter."

Joseph gave a concerned look. "What happened to Lorelei?" His question came with sincerity this time, evident that Joseph was beginning to believe Mr. Christkindl's story. Joseph's well-known emotionless poker face could not conceal his divulgence this time, and Mr. Christkindl was quick to pick up on it. The chubby old man made himself more comfortable, sinking deeper in his chair, and rested his feet on the ottoman in front of him. Mr. Christkindl reached down, loosened his belt by one more hole, giving room for his stomach to expand ever so slightly. "What happened to Lorelei you ask? Come with me back to the war."

The ruthless German soldier eventually caught up to Lorelei, tackling her to the ground separating Loelei from her mother. That tenacious young woman put up a fierce fight, rewarding the Nazi with quite a shiner to his left eye. In frustration the soldier pulled a pistol from his leather holster, shoving the end of the barrel deep into her ribs. Lorelei knew she no longer had the upper hand and was forced to surrender.

Angered by the incident, her Nazi captor was determined to have her executed for resisting arrest. "Get moving." the soldier demanded. Marching her to his assigned company, Soldat Schäfer didn't waste any time reporting her actions to the commanding officer. "Soldat Schäfer reporting sir with prisoner." The irate Nazi blustered out to the commander, gripping Lorelei's arm firmly and digging his pistol tip a little further into her side." The commander remained sitting at his desk and peered over his glasses towards Lorelei and Schäfer. "Prisoner, eh? Very well, let's hear your report." Soldat Schäfer gave a well thought out report, fabricated with lies in order to win his case. Lorelei had interrupted his false report numerous times before her argument was silenced with a firm slap on her cheek. Ultimately the commander became her jury and judge, and the hasty execution order was given and confirmed when it was finally discovered that she was a Jew. The commanding officer grabbed Lorelei's left arm, thanked Soldat Schäfer for his fine work, and called a young soldier standing guard outside his office over to him.

"Youngman, I want you to transport this Jewish filth to the KL Warschau extermination camp immediately." A grin stretched across the commander's hardened face. "Gunter, I want you to leave Hanz behind on this assignment," he continued. "It's time to become a leader and prove your worth. Take her all the way to the front door of the

KL Warschau camp. Deny her mercy, and do not show an ounce of kindness to her. They are subhuman after all. This Fräulein does not deserve any more respect than a bug under my boot." The officer peeled the black leather glove off his right hand, striking her face with it. Her left cheek seared with fire and unquenchable fury raged in her gut. "Go, get on your way. Get her out of my sight!" the office protested.

Gunter yanked the red-faced Lorelei out of the officer's sight and forced her to remove her shoes. "Now let's see you escape walking barefoot down the country road," Gunter jeered. "So, filthy Fräulein, are you not the liébling of Kristoff? You know … are you not his dirty Jewish girlfriend?"

Lorelei did not respond. She stopped in her steps and stared blankly at the ground. Her anger was now at boiling point, welling up inside her like lava ready to spew out of the top of a volcano. Gunter lifted his right boot off the ground and pushed it firmly in her lower back, giving her a good shove and knocked her off balance. "Get going, Fräulein, you don't want to be late for your execution. You know, Lorelei, Kristoff isn't the same anymore. He hates Jews. He told me the other night that he hadn't heard from you in a long time and hoped you had suffered a painful death. He never really liked you. He can't believe he ever befriended you in the first place."

Deep down Lorelei wanted it not to be true. She would not let Gunter have the satisfaction of getting inside her head. Gunter was relentless. He continued to think of lie after lie to degrade her and crush any spirit of hope or love left in her.

"Hey, I just remembered something. Your precious Kristoff is actually just down the road on patrol. I wonder what he'll do when he learns that I found you? I don't think you believe me, Lorelei. He really hates you. To prove this to you and to prove his loyalty to the Führer, we will not walk to KL Warschau. No, I think I'll let Kristoff execute you instead. If you're lucky, we might even bury you in a shallow unmarked grave."

Gunter didn't believe his own words about Kristoff. Gunter suspected all along that Kristoff still loved Lorelei and that Kristoff had a soft spot for Jewish people. His plan would accomplish his heinous design. Kristoff would be forced to kill Lorelei. If he didn't, it would expose him as a Jewish loving trader. *If he was exposed,* Gunter thought to himself, *both Kristoff and Lorelei would be swiftly executed.* In Gunter's mind it was a win-win situation.

Gunter and Lorelei changed course and headed west toward the area Kristoff was last known to be patrolling. The rough road was painful on Lorelei's feet and the sharp pebbles cut her feet like shards of glass. Intermittent trails of blood could be seen in her footprints. Gunter relished the thought of her in pain and each painful step filled him with satisfaction. A motor's rumble caught the attention of Gunter. He stopped and looked back from the direction they had been walking. The sunlight reflected off the windshield of the approaching vehicle. He squinted his eyes, hoping to help him identify what was heading his way. "Ah, look here. It looks like a leichter panzerspähwagen is approaching. Clearly a reconnaissance scout car is interested in us. Wait here, filth, while I explain to them where I am taking you to." Gunter wiped the sweat from his brow and straightened his shirt.

The armored eight-wheeled vehicle's brakes screeched as the driver stepped down on the heavy brake pedal. Instantly Gunter's arm whipped forward in a salute. "Heil Hitler," he greeted the goggled man in the gun turret. The gunner stood up, returned a salute, and removed his goggles. Gunter let out a gasp and his stomach lurched.

"Gunter, is that you?"

Gunter nodded.

"Where are you going with that young lady?" Kristoff asked.

Lorelei stood a pace away and refused to look up at the men. Her dirty bangs covered her tear-filled eyes.

Gunter quietly cleared his throat. "Ja," came his boyish reply. "Ja, Kristoff, it's me Gunter."

Kristoff bent over and shouted to the driver. "Eckerd, turn off the motor. It's Gunter. Let's take a break and visit."

The rumbling motor rattled to a stop, and both men hopped off the scout vehicle. Lorelei stood frozen in her blood footprints.

"What gives, Gunter?" asked Kristoff. "Where are you taking that young woman? When did you become a prisoner transporter?"

Gunter glared back at Kristoff. "And when did they let you become a gunner on a scout vehicle, Kristoff? Clearly you don't have what it takes to be inside a real tank."

Eckerd cleared his throat and turned his head so Gunter couldn't see him speak. "Kristoff, why did we stop to talk to him?"

Kristoff furrowed his brow. "I don't know why I stopped. Something inside me told me to stop. I can't explain it."

Eckerd shrugged his shoulders. "Fair enough. You and your inner voice and feelings again." Eckerd knew that Kristoff had a long history of listening to an inner guiding voice that seemed to guide him in his journey.

"I have something you can help me with, Kristoff," Gunter said. "I've been instructed to take this rebel Jew to be executed. We can save our legs and just do it here. Why don't you do the honor for us?"

Kristoff understood what Gunter was up to. He now found himself in a precarious situation. "I thought you said you were ordered to take her to be executed, not to execute her. I haven't been given any orders to do so, and I'll not be held accountable for breaking rules of command." With this response, Kristoff felt secure and safe.

"Turn around, dirty Jew!" Gunter ordered his prisoner. "Let's get a good look at you before we shoot you."

"I'm not going to shoot her. I told you, Gunter."

Suddenly the woman turned and faced the men. Her dirty moist bangs covered her face as she tilted her head downward. Gunter grabbed his pistol from his leather holster and placed it to her head.

"Gunter, I said no!" thundered Kristoff.

Gunter ignored him and pressed the barrel of the pistol to the bridge of her nose. Sweeping her greasy bangs to the side with his pistol, he exposed her face.

"Lorelei!" Kristoff said.

Gunter looked back, hoping to catch him in his trap. Kristoff walked down and shoved Gunter's muscular body out of the way. "I knew it, Kristoff! You're a Jewish loving traitor and deserve to die."

Kristoff glanced at Gunter, then zeroed in on Lorelei. Raising his hand high in the air, he struck her across her face with his open palm, knocking her to the ground.

"Get up, Fräulein. I have been waiting for this moment for quite some time and Gunter is right. You do deserve to die.

Kristoff grabbed Lorelei by the hair on the back of her head and forced her to her feet. Tears streamed down her face as she pleaded with Kristoff for mercy.

"Gunter, give me your pistol," Kristoff demanded. Gunter's trembling hand stretched forward, and Kristoff ripped the pistol from it. "I'm finishing this once and for all. Both of you. Go get in the panzerspähwagen and wait for me!" he shouted, pointing at Gunter and Eckerd.

The two young soldiers were so struck with such fear that they beelined it back to the scout vehicle never looking back. Neither one of them had ever witnessed Kristoff so violent or angry before. "He must have truly snapped," a half-winded Eckerd said as he clambered up the panzerspähwagen behind a frightened Gunter.

"March toward the trees," Kristoff ordered Lorelei as he walked behind her. He continuously shoved her in the back until they were out of sight of the panzerspähwagen and well obscured by the tree line. Once out of view of Gunter and Eckerd, he stopped abruptly and demanded her to kneel down on the ground, keep her hands behind her back, and not to say a word. Screaming out in protest, Lorelei refused to kneel. Instead, she instinctively drove her fist as hard as she could into Kristoff's nose, sending a flood of blood out of his nostrils and over his chin.

"Stop this nonsense and kneel down, Lorelei. Don't make me tell you again!" Kristoff shouted. Firmly gripping her arm to prevent her escape, he once again demanded her to kneel before him.

Lorelei sank to her knees in front of Kristoff in defeat. Her cold muddied hands trembled as she stared emotionless in front of her, refusing to look away. Kristoff clenched the wooden pistol grip in his hand and raised the barrel level to her head. He paused for a moment, staring down at his target. Holding his breath, he squeezed the cold metal trigger twice rapidly. The reverberation of the gunshots echoed off the surrounding trees and rumbled over the hill behind him. A ghostly smoke column fluttered from the tip of the hot barrel, and the unmistakable sound of a lifeless body fell to the earth in front of him.

Acting quickly, Kristoff dropped to his knees, caught hold of Lorelei's dress sleeve, and tore the well-worn material off her shoulder with ease. Sliding his Hitlerjugend knife from its leather sheath, he gasped her long dirty hair and chopped a thick eight-inch length of braided hair from the back of her head. Kristoff then began ripping the tattered dress sleeve into several slender strips and laid them next to Lorelei's severed lock of hair. Holding the braid tightly, he secured the bundle of hair together with the makeshift cords from the strips of torn dress sleeve. Using the now tightly braided hair like a napkin, Kristoff wiped the blood from his nose and chin.

"Wake up, Lorelei. Wake up," Kristoff whispered as he shook her limp body vigorously. "Wake up already!" Lorelei scrunched her eyelids tightly together, then began blinking wildly.

"What just happened?" Lorelei asked, confused.

"You fainted the moment I squeezed the trigger," Kristoff said. "I wasn't going to kill you. I shot the ground behind you. I had to think fast, Lorelei. I know this must have been so scary for you not knowing my real intent. Striking you with my hand earlier was the hardest thing I have ever had to do," he said. "I'm so sorry for all the things I did. I may never forgive myself for laying a hand on you, but now they think you're dead, that I shot you, and I have a bundle of bloody hair to prove it. I had to play the part if we want to continue to fight against tyranny." "Kristoff, this was very scary. I was so frightened. I truly thought you were going to kill me. Why did you have to do it this way?" Lorelei said with her face buried in her trembling hands. "If I didn't do this, we both would be on our way to be executed. Run away, far away. If this war ever ends, meet me where it all began for us. I'll find you. I promise." He grabbed her face in his hand, and his thick thumb wiped the tears from her face. He softly pressed his lips to hers, pushed her away, and said, "Run!" Lorelei stumbled backwards a few steps then spun around in the opposite direction. Jogging a few paces away she turned back for one last look. Tears drenched her face and filled her eyelids as she watched Kristof walking away. "I love you." Her whispered words over quivering lips never reached his ears.

Trudging back to the awaiting panzerspähwagen, Kristoff collapsed on the turret floor behind the 20 mm autocannon. He dropped his sweaty face into his hands, and rewatched the traumatizing event flickering in his mind like a picture show replaying in slow motion. No matter how tightly he closed his eyes or clenched his jaw, it could not remedy the indelible image now repeating in his head. He knew he had just saved Lorelei's life, and this was the only peace he could draw upon. Kristoff cracked open his eyes and stared down blankly at the tethered bloodied hair clutched in his trembling right hand.

"What's that in your hand, Kris?" asked Eckerd.

He didn't respond. He rolled the locks of hair back and forth between his thumb and index finger.

"That's Lorelei's hair, Eckerd!" exclaimed Gunter, who was now staring wide-eyed at Kristoff. "You did it! You actually did it. You killed her."

Kristoff scowled. "Of course I did it, Gunter. I did what you couldn't do yourself. You talk big, but when it comes right down to it, you don't have what it takes."

Gunter recoiled at the truth of his accusation. Kristoff's furrowed brow signaled warfare, and Gunter retreated to the driver's seat, murmuring under his breath.

Eckerd's chin quivered. "How could you do this? What happened?"

Kristoff tilted his head and peered at Eckerd. The wink of an eye was all it took to tell Eckerd the truth. Grinning, Eckerd slipped out of sight and joined Gunter below.

12

The Lonely Boys

Lorelei felt her hands shaking violently as her nails dug deep into the dry bark of the fallen tree in front of her. The rattled young woman intently watched the heavy panzerspähwagen creep down the potholed road and out of sight. It's deep rumbling motor could still be heard in the distance until, at last, the entire valley fell mute all around her. Lorelei let go of a large tree branch providing her concealment and collapsed to the ground.

Staring heavenward, she examined each gray-laced, puffy, white cloud floating by without a care. Lorelei rested on the ground pensively and faltered at the idea of standing up or moving. For at that very moment, her little world was at peace. She was finally in control of herself once again. There was no one there to chase her, ordering her around or threatening to take her life. Lying motionless on the ground, all was as it should be, in her silent serenity. By and by, cloud after passing cloud, her racing heart normalized, her breathing slowed, and her hands steadied once again.

Lorelei was unsure how long she had been lying on ground and it wasn't until a squadron of passing fighter planes soaring overhead in stunning formation broke her impromptu meditation.

"Back to reality" she said quietly, as she sat up and scanned her surroundings. To her back was the road Kristoff traveled. On either side of her, large fields stretched for miles, sprinkled with vegetation and an occasional cluster of trees. In front of her was the long stretch of road that led to the city of Warsaw. Her mother undoubtedly had traveled that route in recent days. *Perhaps*, she thought, *if I'm swift enough, and with a lot of luck, I could happen upon my mother en route.* Determined to reunite with her mother, she made a beeline for the trees that lined the roadside toward Warsaw.

Traveling alone, though frightening, did have its benefits. She could move quite quickly and finding hiding places was much easier for one than looking for a place for two. Lorelei picked wild berries to eat when she could find them, and a time or two she was found some rations discarded in abandoned Nazi campsites. Miraculously, she remained undetected by sleeping during the day and traveling at night. Every day before morning's light, she would stack piles of branches under a cluster of trees far from the road and create a camouflaged canopy to rest in. This routine repeated itself day after day until she approached the outskirts of the city, at which point Lorelei had to become more resourceful. Soon she found herself hiding under the floorboards of abandoned buildings or in recesses of rubble. Often the broken water pipes provided enough water to refill a discarded canteen she obtained along the way.

Several nights of observing and hiding out in Warsaw revealed to her that Nazi soldiers continually patrolled the streets, making it impossible to continue any further towards the Warsaw Zoo. Lorelei abandoned her plan, feeling it was too risky to remain hiding inside the city and subsequently determined it would be necessary to leave later that night after the routine Nazi patrol passed by around 8:00 p.m.

Patiently waiting the hour to leave, Lorelei observed the streets from the confines of her hiding place. Most of the city's citizens avoided the streets and public places once the sun set. It was unusual to see individuals in the streets, other than those wearing the feared Nazi uniform. For most, safety in any quantity was rare and mildly felt during the daylight.

The eight o'clock hour approached and like clockwork, a group of four Nazi soldiers patrolled through the street looking for anyone breaking curfew. From a distance, Lorelei watched as the men peered inside the front windows of stores and flashed lights inside some of the collapsed buildings or vacant houses. Their patrols as usual, did not yield results, and the four men rounded the street corner and out of sight.

A short time after the men departed, a small group of young men ducked into a bombed-out shell of a building at the edge of town. Crawling out from under her rubble-covered dwelling, Lorelei scurried across the street and followed the group of boys into the building. Three of the perimeter walls remained upright, the fourth fell inward collapsing on what appeared to be a cashier's counter. The entire store had been looted, leaving only fractured bricks, crushed mortar, and dust. Peeking around the corner of the wall, Lorelei made brief eye contact with a dirty faced young man sitting on a stack of bricks he used as a makeshift chair.

"Who's there? Come on now, show yourself!" a commanding voice beckoned from the back of the building.

"I need a word with you," Lorelei replied timidly. "I'm looking for my parents. They are hiding in the Warsaw Zoo."

"Sounds like your parents are zebras or perhaps a long-necked giraffe," said one young man. "Ain't a thing there but wild animals."

"Silence, Amos. Leave her be." A sooty haired boy of about sixteen sat up from his bricked chair and stepped forward. "Name is Raimund. These are my boys. Lost our parents and now we're family. My apologies for Amos. We're still working on his manners." Raimund motioned for his buddies to come forward. "Come on out. You don't want to frighten her."

One by one, each boy emerged until all six dirty-faced boys were standing in front of Lorelei. The largest of them all, Raimund towered over the rest by at least a head or two, and it was no wonder he was the leader. His tangled black hair looked as if hadn't seen a comb in ages, but it paired nicely with his ripped trouser and stained khaki shirt. His appearance was rough, but his soft brown eyes and straight teeth made him very approachable.

"Don't listen to Amos. We know what you're talking about. Tunnels under the zoo are a well-kept secret. I knew you were one of us the moment you mentioned the zoo." Pointing down at the pintsized boy on the left, Raimund continued, "See Dominic over there? He is our best runner in the sewer tunnels. Gives the rats a good run for their money, given his size and all." The undersized boy's cheeks flushed, and he flashed a crooked toothed smile in Raimund's direction.

Lorelei leaded towards Raimund. "I would like to know if Martha or Albert Blumenfeld are down there. Is there any way to find out?"

Raimund signaled to Dominic, who darted through a broken window and out of sight. "He'll be back in a flash. Dependable that one is. Have a seat. Pull up a piece of rubble." The boys plopped down to the dusty ground and Lorelei sat lightly on a large chunk of cement.

"So, what is it you boys do anyways?"

"We run information to groups hiding out. It is a way we feel that we can contribute as well as fight back. See, we're all orphans after the first bombing."

"Family we are," a round-faced boy in the middle broke in. "We call ourselves the Lonely Boys."

"We're on our way to deliver some rations to a house outside of the city. There are two to three families hiding in the attic, and we keep them fed. It's rewarding to see them light up when we arrive. They have taken refuge with a small family. The owner has walled-up secret passages and made it undetectable to anyone inspecting. It's quite the sight. You really should come see it." Raimund looked down at his feet and drew a circle with the toe of his worn brown leather shoe. "So, how long have you been looking for your folks, anyway?"

Lorelei slouched. "It's been several weeks, I gather. Several difficult weeks."

Dirt and crushed mortar rolled down a large pile behind Amos. "See there! Ain't he fast?"

Dominic panted, and brushed off the rubble from his trousers.

"What did you find out?" asked a twiggy boy seated next to Amos.

"Gone they are. Apparently, they waited for some time but an opportunity came up to leave and they had no choice. It was one of those now or never moments." Dominic collapsed on the dirty floor and scribbled in the dust with his finger. "Loads of people are making a run for it at night you know. Your folks left with two other families toward Denmark in hopes of getting to Sweden. We've heard that the Danes are secretly sending their Jewish countrymen to Sweden by boat. Our hope has been that they can send a few more from Warsaw that way as well. The men down in the tunnels told me that your folks departed about a week or so ago." Dominic returned his finger to the dust and pushed the dirt into small piles. "Hope they make it."

Raimund lifted his gaze towards Lorelei and spoke in a soft tone, "They'll make it to Sweden just fine. If Lorelei here is any indication of who they are, they're probably stepping off the boat and onto foreign soil this very minute." Lorelei glanced at Raimund, slumping her shoulders slightly.

"I'm coming with you to that house you spoke of earlier. Maybe I can't be with my family at this moment, but perhaps I can help others. My best hope is that this war will end soon, and then I'll make my own way to Sweden. I just pray that I'll see my parents again."

The group of young men scrambled to their feet and hustled to the side door. Forcing the door open, one after another they contorted through the narrow opening, spilling out into the alleyway. "Come quickly. The night patrol will be back through this area soon," Raimund said. Meandering through mazes of rubble and collapsed buildings, the gang made their way out of Warsaw to a farm a few miles outside of town.

The wooden framed farmhouse was a welcoming contrast to the large structures and living arrangements they had come to know in the city. The farm was no longer in operation, and where once the house was surrounded by fertile fields, now was bordered in barren land neglected by a plow. Several birch trees hugged the house. Its stretching limbs tickled the walls in the breeze. The covered porch was clean and well cared for, and the few potted plants out front gave life to the home. Glancing upward, Lorelei noted a warm flickering glow from the upper dormer window.

"That's the sign," Raimund said, pointing at the light in the dormer window. "They're waiting for us. Come around back."

The teenager made his way to a back window and tapped on the lower glass window with a small pebble. He paused for thirty seconds and repeated. The window slid open, and a weathered hand reached out. Raimund placed his gunny sack of provisions into the hand. The hand pulled the food inside, then returned the empty bag back to Raimund. The window started to close when Raimund thrust his hand inside, stopping it. Leaning in, Raimund whispered something and leaned back out. The window closed and latched.

"Go to the back door, Lorelei. Gerwin will take care of you from here."

Standing on her toes, Lorelei pressed her soft lips to Raimund's warm cheek. "Thank you, Raimund. I'll not forget what you have done for me."

Raimund's eyes crinkled at the corners, and Lorelei dropped back to her heels. The back door cracked open, and the weathered hand reached out once again. Lorelei clasped hands with the farmer and stepped inside.

13

Die Eule

It didn't take long for the news of what had happened between Kristoff and Lorelei to spread like a raging fire inside camp. Thanks to Hanz (the camp gossip) and his devotion to Gunter, not only did all the soldiers and officers hear about it, but the story also became more and more embellished. It now included Gunter saving Kristoff from being shot by Lorelei. Gunter embraced Hanz's story to weasel his way into favoritism among his commanding officers with the hopes of rank promotion. Kristoff didn't attempt to correct the story; instead, he embraced it, allowing it to build the facade of his loyalties. Hanz and Gunter didn't realize that their storytelling only helped Kristoff.

It was true—the fictitious story did provide opportunities for Kristoff to lead soldiers on training exercises and gave him certain access to some classified information. It was a general feeling among his comrades that Kristoff could be trusted over any other soldier around. It was said that words of his supposed heroic event had made it to the Fuehrer's desk for review and a possible consideration to receive a medal was in the works. This news fueled Gunter's anger even more. Once again, he was left standing in the shadows of Kristoff's greatness.

Today was different from most routine days for Kristoff. On this occasion, he found himself sitting in a leather padded armchair next to a boat-sized oval conference table. Several military maps covered the polished wooden surface underneath. Tiny Nazi flags fixed to miniature flag poles dotted the map, indicating locations of troops and advancing infantry. The stale dimly lit room reeked of dirty ashtrays. Its only source of light was from a single overhead hanging light bulb. Kristoff faced the frosted square-windowed door that had remained slightly open, allowing the stern voices of the adjacent room to be heard. Outbound coded messages were being broadcasted, though the details were drowned out by the constant slapping of typewriter keys smashing the heavy paper with every stroke.

"Kristoff, sorry to keep you waiting." A short, round man with squinty eyes and three chins, waddled into the room. The man was loud, smelled of alcohol, and white pastry crumbs sprinkled his dark ribboned uniform.

Kristoff sprang to his feet. "Heil Hitler," he said. The swine-like man returned the salute.

"Please sit, Christkindl," Oberführer Karl Berndt said. "I'm sorry to make you wait, but I was, uh…um… engaged in something that I couldn't get away from very easily."

A jelly Danish and Vodka by the smell of it, Kristoff thought.

"I came to discuss with you about a special mission of sorts we need you to help us with," he said. "Close the door, junger soldat."

Kristoff leaned to his right and pushed the door gently until the latch clicked. The tipsy man let out a small burp and resumed his mission briefing. "We recently intercepted information that someone referred to as Die Eule, an informant working for the rebellious Polish Jews, will be meeting at a known rendezvous point. Die Eule has been true to his name. He is a quiet owl observing his surroundings and makes his attack in the shadows of the night. Someone on the inside is providing Eule with military plans and our objectives. He has been tipping off Jews that are holding up in hiding places of our planned raids. Subsequently, he is foiling our progress, and many German soldiers have died because his warnings allowed Jewish rebels to take up arms in defense of Poland."

Kristoff tried to hide the look of confusion. "Why me? Why would you need me to help? What can I possibly do?"

The tubby officer pulled a half-smoked cigar from the inner pocket of his overcoat and poked the soggy end of it in his mouth. Striking a wooden matchstick, the orangey-blue flames licked the distal end of the stogie, and a small puff of smoke wafted upward toward the ceiling. "Christkindl, it has been said that a young Jewish woman had taken a fancy to you, but in your cunning way, you made her believe that you liked her back, only to lead her to her execution by your own hands." A puff of smoke escaped his mouth and nostrils with every word. "This is quite honorable, Kristoff. Your story was even mentioned by the Führer himself at a recent officers banquet. You are really starting to make a name for yourself. Da, junger soldat…. making a name at such a young age."

Kristoff tapped his thumbs on the table rhythmically like a steady drum player in a concert. He flashed a quick glance at the Oberführer, then back down on his percussive thumbs. "What's my mission, sir? How can I serve the Führer?"

Oberführer Berndt plopped down in the rickety chair next to Kristoff. Leaning in, he whispered, "We're going to catch Die Eule in a trap. This is where you come in. We have a report of two families hiding in the outskirts of Warsaw. These Jews have been smuggling in food and medical supplies to the Ghetto holding the Polish Jews. As you likely can recall, recently, German civilian occupation authorities required all of Warsaw's Jews to identify themselves by wearing white armbands marked with a blue Star of David and to move into a designated area, which we successfully sealed off from the rest of the city. The Oberführer pulled the cigar from his mouth, rolled it around between his fingers as if inspecting it, grinned and gently placed it back in his mouth.

"After sealing off the city, we confiscated property, and forced the men into labor. We have only allowed small rations to the Jews to keep them alive. We are aware that some not loyal to our cause feel that we are not providing enough food and are somehow sneaking in additional rations, medical supplies, and even weapons. Oberführer Berndt stood and began clumsily pacing the floor, knocking over an empty bottle of Vodka off of his desk, shattering it in pieces.

Unaware of the broken bottle under his shoes, he continued in his rant, "In the beginning of this year, our SS and police units returned to Warsaw, with the intent of deporting the remaining ghetto Jews to our labor camps in Lublin. When we returned, we encountered a great deal of resistance. Somehow, they found out that our SS would deport them to Treblinka for execution, so they began to resist our efforts of deportation.

The commander wobbled on his heels back towards Kristoff just as a belch erupted from his oversized lips. "Pardon me." he said, covering his mouth with his hand. "Where was I?" He said scratching his sweat beaded head. "Oh right, we also discovered that small arms had been smuggled into the ghetto by the 2 families that I spoke of earlier. In our efforts, we did round many jews, but we withdrew because of the resistance and danger to our own soldiers.

Oberführer Berndt turned back to his desk and sat down once again. "A few months ago, we began deporting the remaining Jews, however the ghetto had successfully organized resistance to our forces and our well-armed SS had sustained significant casualties.

Kristoff leaned back in his chair, and interlaced his fingers, resting them on the tabletop. "If this family is such a problem by supplying the

Jewish resistance, why didn't you storm in with the SS and eliminate them?" asked Kristoff.

Oberführer Berndt sucked in more smoke from his smoldering cigar and continued, "We discovered the identity of the families providing rations. However, we haven't ordered a raid, as of yet. I felt that this would provide the perfect opportunity to flush someone we call the Elusive Die Eule out of his hiding spot, and when he does, we will capture him and bring him to swift justice. I can only imagine what the Führer will do to him. I'm certain it will be a slow painful death." The smoky overweight man wrung his sweaty fingers together over and over anticipating his victory. "Christkindl, you are the most trusted soldier we have. We know you're not responsible for leaking military plans, and we're also certain you're not the Elusive Die Eule. The plan is to have you in the observation point of the target twenty-four hours prior to releasing the news to the selected SS team that will be assigned to the raid. We are confident that someone in our offices has been leaking the information to Die Eule, and this will draw him out and right into our hands."

"But what if Die Eule doesn't show up? What if the leak isn't in our office? What will happen to the family at that point?" Kristoff asked.

Oberführer Berndt stood up from his chair and looked down at Kristoff. "Then your mission will then be a body recovery. Regardless, if Die Eule shows up or not, these families will be executed on the spot." The Oberführer walked out of the room, paused, and then stated to Kristoff, "You leave tomorrow night. Be ready." Cigar smoke faded the round man's silhouette following him as he marched down the hall and out of sight.

Kristoff remained in the room alone for the next twenty minutes replaying the conversation in his mind. *Die Eule, wow... they actually assigned a codename, the Elusive Owl, that's pretty slick,* he thought.

Kristoff was concerned. He knew that he was actually the Elusive

Die Eule. For several years, Kristoff had been foiling executions and had saved countless innocent Jewish lives by thwarting military and police raids. His commanding officers trusted him and all because of his well-planned masquerade from the moment he joined the Hitlerjugend. No amount of top-secret information was ever too far or too secure for Kristoff. He used this trust to his advantage and innumerable lives had been spared.

Later that night, Kristoff lay awake in his bed formulating a plan to maintain his secret identity, yet at the same time, protect the families from being raided. *This is not going to be easy*, he thought. *If I tip off the family, but do not have an alibi for myself, I'll be discovered and found to be guilty of treason.* The solution did not come right away for Kristoff this time, and his plan was as full of holes as a moth-infested wool jacket. The only solution he could come up with was to take his place in hiding and purposely be discovered by making too much noise. *Hopefully they'll see me and take off running out the back door. This would solve the problem as far as I can see. They would be safe, and I would not be discovered.* Kristoff rolled over, tucking his pillow under his head.

"There are many variables that could go wrong, but this is the best I can come up with," he mumbled.

"What's that you say? You awake, Kristoff?" Eckerd asked from the bunk a few feet away.

"Go back to bed, Eckerd. It's nothing." Kristoff pulled the covers higher over his shoulder, covering his head.

"Well, you sure are mumbling a lot for someone with NOTHING wrong."

Kristoff felt Eckerd's frustration with every uttered syllable. Up to this point, Kristoff never kept a secret from his best friend, and he felt terrible, but he couldn't risk his friend's life in this situation. Eckerd remained quiet the remainder of the night, probably sulking in his bed.

The day of Kristoff's secret departure arrived, and he found himself once again sitting in a troop transport bouncing down the back roads. This time, however, he sat completely alone on a secret mission. Earlier that morning, he had been re-briefed regarding his mission plans, and his required supplies had been organized tightly into his heavy backpack. Oberführer Berndt was overseeing this secret mission and wanted to make sure that Kristoff returned safely with his prized information. To ensure his safe return, he insisted that Kristoff be armed with a Maschinenpistole 40. The MP40 submachine gun, in Oberführer Berndt's mind, gave him plenty of firepower to protect himself if something were to go wrong.

The truck tires rolled to a stop and the driver reached his arm through the open window pounding on the metal door signaling Kristoff to get out. Slinging the strap of his MP40 over his right shoulder, he stepped down off the covered truck and ducked behind the roadside shrubbery near a rickety abandoned barn. Crouching low he watched the truck speed away, disappearing into the setting sun.

Kristoff had been dropped half a kilometer from his target, allotting him sufficient time to approach the house unseen. Reaching into the outside pocket of his backpack, he retrieved a pocket-sized folded map. Carefully expanding the map, he traced a thick penciled line with his index finger from his current position to an x-marked structure circled in red. A business-sized black-and-white photo of the house was paperclipped to the map. He studied the photo one last time before replacing it back into his pack along with his collapsed map. Squatting behind the bushes, he scanned the countryside with his binoculars. Peaked-frame farmhouses and abandoned barns dotted the rolling hills in all directions, and the once fertile fields were now left hauntingly neglected. A wooden slate fence in various states of disrepair stretched along the right side of the road and encompassed the once productive farm that Kristoff was now using as a temporary hiding spot.

He spent the next hour and a half observing how eerily quiet this village actually was. No animals, active farming, or laughter of children could be heard. Life in this village had been snuffed out by the brutality of war. At length the evening sun melted away at a snail's pace, casting ever lengthening shadows on the cool damp ground he was sitting on. Soon the night sky rested upon the terrain, darkening all of his surroundings, making him feel more marooned. The night sky was void of a moon, and the wispy clouds floating high in the sky intermittently obscured the starlight, providing Kristoff the cloak of darkness he desired.

Feeling safe and undetected, Kristoff fetched his equipment and cautiously made his way down the dirt road toward his assignment. Each turn of the road replayed the same story of abandoned farms and houses incinerated at the hands of the ruthless Nazi party whose uniform he was wearing. This was not a safe place to be a lone soldier in an area ravaged by his own army. If anyone from this village had survived, Kristoff would be a walking target for revenge. Kristoff now comprehended why Oberführer Berndt insisted on him being armed with such a destructive weapon for a simple observation mission. The Oberführer wanted to protect his informant, and it was unmistakable that he had knowledge of the recent attacks on this blameless farming community and would stop at nothing to discover who was the Elusive Die Eule.

Even though Kristoff excelled in cartography at school, the journey to the observation point took longer than he had anticipated. Sneaking behind the shield of shrubbery and lurking in the night's shadows proved to be quite time consuming.

"At last!" he said to himself. "I made it." He recognized the house from the small photo attached to his map. A flickering orange flame was casting a warm glow in the front room of the house and silhouetted shadows of small children darting in and out graced the window curtain like an old-time picture show. This was the first sight of life detected in the area since the time Kristoff was dropped off earlier in the evening.

The presence of little children in the home did not sit well with Kristoff as he recounted the words of Oberführer Berndt: the family would be executed on the spot. Kristoff determined right then and there that he wouldn't let this happen at any cost. He hunkered down thirty meters away from the house, concealing him from view behind a large stack of firewood. *I'll need to wait until morning for my opportunity to reveal myself and alert the family of my presence. Hopefully, they'll run at the sight of my uniform*, he thought.

Kristoff plucked rations of bread and a small piece of chocolate from his pack, then leaned his back against the dry stacked logs. Popping a torn chunk of bread in his mouth, he stared off into the darkness, rehearsing his plan for the next morning.

Snap!

The unmistakable sound of a dry twig being crushed under a boot came from the darkness, only a stone's throw away from where he sat. Kristoff held deathly still and listened more intently. Several minutes passed, his pounding heartbeat filling his ears, making it impossible to discern the distant noises.

He strained his ears even more, trying to pick up any noise being carried on the cool night's breeze. *I'm just paranoid*, he thought, then his mind began to wonder. *What if it is a villager stalking him like prey, or an American Soldier lining up his iron sights to make a clean shot, or what if the family he is spying on is circling around him ready to attack?* His heart rate surged with the thoughts of a pending onslaught.

Crack!

A brittle twig fractured again, breaking the unnerving silence. Kristoff's face flushed with fear.

He was not alone.

14

The Sacrificial Plan

Cloaked eyes stared at Kristoff from the dim forest tree line. *Why aren't they attacking?* he asked himself. *There is more than meets the eye here. This must be a setup. But why?* He continued picking his brain for the solution, reviewing in his mind the prior meeting he had with Oberführer Berndt, trying to find a connection to him and the person hiding in the dark. Finally, it dawned on him. *I must be the one under scrutiny here. They are secretly observing me to see how I will react to the order to execute a Jewish family. Oberführer Berndt must have been suspicious that I am Die Eule and is setting me up. He sent someone here to get evidence that I am the one tipping the Jews of Nazi attacks.* He slumped down lower behind the wood stack feeling very unsettled.

The late night dragged on into the early morning hours, and Kristoff was unable to sleep a wink. He feared all night long that he would be overrun or attacked in his sleep by the unknown onlooker. This had been the longest night he could remember in recent memory, and he was on high alert, very aware that someone was observing his every move. A soft yellowish-blue glow gradually appeared over the distant eastern mountaintops stretching its golden rays across the blue sky, highlighting the surrounding valley. Wildlife began to spring to life in all directions the moment the early morning sunbeams breached the tree line. Gradually large columns of yellow sunlight began to grace the dark green treetops, and landed on Kristoff's face, warming his nose and cheeks.

In the distance, birds could be seen launching from the moist ground cover taking early low-level flights in the dim skyline while field rabbits emerged from dirt burrows pressing their twitching noses into the cool damp vegetation. Morning had arrived. Coupled with this was Kristoff's need of a delicate balancing act by making himself known to the unsuspecting family, though not revealing his true intent to frighten the family into running, while yet preserving his hidden identity and ultimately saving innocent Jewish lives.

Kristoff positioned himself behind the wood pile and spied nervously over the top of a weathered stack of logs. His new position provided an unblocked view of the front door and limited view of the sides of the small houses. Surveying the house and the surrounding area, Kristoff could hear anxious movement disturbing the brittle underbrush, a stone's throw away from him and reacting to his every move.

The flickering orange glow of a candle illuminated the front window of the house. The tattered drape was pulled to the side in a sweeping motion and a dark silhouette peered out the window. Kristoff believed that someone was checking to see if it was clear to exit the home undetected. The window drape dropped back into its resting position, and Kristoff heard the door locks tumble open. With some effort from the inside, the door opened slightly inward, and once again a silhouette could be seen peering through the gap in the doorway. Kristoff's face flushed and his heart raced inside his chest.

The door gap widened, and a slender male figure squeezed through the narrow opening to the cool outside air. The figure whipped his hands behind him and placed both of his palms on his lower back, and pushed forward while arching his upper back backwards into a good morning stretch. His apparent daily routine proved to Kristoff that the man was unaware he was being watched from the woodpile. In less than no time, two smaller child-size figures emerged from the same gap in the door and approached the man.

Kristoff placed his right hand on a gnarled piece of kindling and gave it a gentle shove away from him. The log slipped off the top of the stack and crashed onto the hardened dirt with a thud. The man whipped his head in Kristoff's direction and stared motionless at the fallen log. Kristoff squared his hat and stood up slowly from behind the stacked wood pile. Reacting to the Nazi uniform, the man reached behind him, pulled something from his waistband, and pointed it in Kristoff's direction. The two children dashed behind the man, creating one large dark silhouette.

Behind Kristoff, heavy feet stomped the ground, crushing brittle twigs. The sounds were racing in his direction. The thunder of boots to his rear were drowned out by the cluster of gunfire exploding behind him, whizzing over his head. A flurry of bullets pelted the front of the house, splintering the wood panels into toothpicks and shattering the front windowpane into fragments. Shards of glass rained down on the flat figures lying facedown on the ground in front of the bullet-riddled house. Kristoff took cover behind the wood pile. Five blasts of gunfire from the nearly motionless man pierced the air, striking the woodpile and embedding hot lead into the logs as well as the distant trees behind Kristoff.

"Don't you dare shoot at me, you filthy Jew!" shouted Gunter, his voice filled with anger as he squeezed off a burst of additional rounds toward his target on the ground.

"No, Gunter! What are you doing?" Kristoff shouted. In a reaction to protect the helpless family, Kristoff jumped to his feet and raced toward the family. Multiple bullets ripped through Kristoff's back the moment he started running, dropping him to his knees. His ears were ringing, and warm liquid ran down his back. Unable to take a breath, Kristoff collapsed to the ground soaking the soil in his blood. Gunter continued to shoot his weapon recklessly at Kristoff as well as in the direction of the family.

Gunter dropped to the ground, took cover behind Kristoff's lifeless body, and continued to exchange fire with the man on the ground. Kristoff's body provided Gunter with protection from several additional bullets that struck the bloody corpse. Cautiously, Gunter pressed his index and middle finger firmly against Kristoff's neck and looked for a pulse. He couldn't find one. Gunter began shaking the lifeless body, commanding Kristoff to get up. It was no use. Gunter's bullets had snuffed out Kristoff's life.

Gunter gripped the lower half of Kristoff's thin oval erkennungsmarke and broke the midline perforation of his dog tag, leaving the upper portion behind for identification of the body. He reached into Kristoff's pocket and retrieved the paper documentation Kristoff had been carrying with him. Kristoff's Soldbuch that contained his military information had been shredded by bullets and drenched in blood. A few more hot leaded slugs whizzed over Gunter's head, reminding him that a battle was still at hand. He sank lower to the ground, further protecting himself behind Kristoff's corpse.

"You idiot, Kristoff! Those bullets were not intended for you!" Gunter said at the lifeless body. "I was to be the hero and kill this family. This is catastrophic. If it's found out that I killed you on my observation only mission, Oberführer Berndt will never promote me and probably worse."

Gunter's mind raced to come up with a way out of his predicament. *I will blame Kristoff's death on the Jews*, he thought. Secure in his deceit, Gunter rattled off a few more rounds of bullets, buying himself enough time to retreat back into the tree line and safely out of sight. Knowing the blood soaked soldbuch was now useless, Gunter discarded the bloody papers under a bush and raced back to his rendezvous point.

Feeling safe, the man and his two children cautiously crawled back in the bullet riddled house and out of sight. Unknown to that family, Kristoff had just sacrificed his own life for theirs. Gathering together his children in his arms, the man took his family and they raced out the back of the house seeking refuge.

If only Kristoff had known who was hiding behind him, he might have prevented this from happening. However, it was now too late. He had failed in his own preconceived plan. Lorelei, Kristoff's mother, and the suffering Jewish people were now on their own. The surrounding woodland fell deathly silent while the morning sun inched up in the sky allowing the golden rays of light to illuminate the deserted house. Unknown to any Nazi soldiers other than Gunter, Kristoff's cold body was abandoned, left behind to decay in the elements.

15

The Bedside Companion

"I've never seen anything like this before!" said the young woman in the recovery ward. "This is getting stranger and stranger by the moment," she continued to murmur under her breath.

Several light brown curly bangs peeked out from underneath the white cap perched on her head, and the long sleeves of her dress had been rolled up, exposing her bony elbows. A clean white apron covered her blue dress and was fastened tightly around her waist, revealing her slender figure. A white broach with a red-painted cross closed her white collar and completed the uniform.

An older woman with matching apparel approached the murmuring nurse. "What is the matter, krankenschwester Vogel?" asked the older woman.

"Ma'am, this man was dropped off this morning with blood-soaked field dressings and multiple bullet hole perforations. We don't know who brought him in. He didn't come in on a medic transport. He was just lying on the ground out front alone. I personally triaged him this morning and was awaiting surgery for his multiple wounds. The thing I can't explain, he never went to surgery. This morning, I was working in the post op recovery ward. I left for a brief moment for supplies, and when I returned, he was there on his bed. There were no post op orders or records of surgery. I have been monitoring his dressings and blood pressure."

"I see nothing wrong with your care," said Hilda. The seasoned nurse peered down at the white-haired wounded soldier lying on his side.

"Correct, but look." The thin nurse pulled back the soiled gauze exposing clean healthy flesh, no scar or perforations. "It's as if the wounds have miraculously healed."

Both white-capped women leaned in closer to inspect the man's back.

"See, as I said. No wounds."

"It's clearly experimental medicine that has been applied by the scientist under the Führer's command. These men are both soldiers and guinea pigs to be tested. We should applaud the scientific discoveries," said the mature nurse.

"Look, his hair is pure white, obviously secondary to experimental medications. Does this soldier have any identification?"

"Ja, he had his erkennungsmarke on him, though the bottom half of the tag had been broken off or purposely removed." Nurse Vogel said. "The name on his erkennungsmarke reads: Nik Kringle."

"I've never seen such pure white hair on a human before. It's very striking, isn't it, Nurse Vogel?"

"Ja, ma'am, it is. Interestingly," Nurse Vogel replied, "he was dropped off at the entry to the hospital with field dressings applied to his back, and we discovered that his only possessions on him at the time is that beautiful gold ring on his right middle finger and a pair of half-moon spectacles in his uniform shirt pocket."

"Half of his dog tag was missing you said?" questioned Nurse Vogel.

Hilda raised her eyebrows and nodded her head in the affirmative, "That means the soldier was……" Nurse Vogel's voice trailed off.

"Yes, left for dead." Hilda interrupted. "It would appear that someone believed he was dead or beyond saving and they removed half the tag in order to record him with casualties."

"How is he currently doing, Nurse Vogel?"

"His blood pressure is stable 110 over 74, and his respirations are 16. His lungs sound clear bilaterally. He is stable at the moment, yet he appears to be unconscious. It is very possible that he is in a coma. When and if he wakes up, I have so many questions," Nurse Volgel said.

"Make sure to keep me posted," the seasoned nurse said as she turned to leave.

"Come with me for a few minutes, Nurse Vogel. I have another patient I want to discuss with you." The two women walked down to the end of the corridor and out of sight.

Kristoff lay in the medical bed motionless. The sounds of the hospital ward felt distant and muffled in his ears. He could hear conversations coming from somewhere in the room, but he didn't recognize the voices and couldn't make out what they were saying. The wounded white-haired young man felt like he was in a dream, fighting to get out, struggling to wake up.

Over the next two hours, the surrounding sounds gradually clarified and with all of his efforts, he made his first attempt to open his eyes. His heavy eyelids were dry, he cracked them open just enough to permit a sliver of white light to enter his pupils. A few rapid blinks was all it took to discover where he was.

A medical ward, he thought. *I must be wounded. But I don't feel any pain.*

Looking over his left shoulder, he could make out some medical supplies piled on a tray next to him. He leaned over with his left hand and grabbed the shiny metal tray, knocking gauze, cotton balls, and a small bottle of alcohol to the floor. Stretching out his hand in front of his face, he angled the smooth metal tray searching for his reflection in his crude mirror.

Well now, that looks like me for certain, he thought as he tilted the tray in all directions, carefully inspecting his face. After a few brief moments, he angled the tray upward to inspect his forehead. *Why does my hair look white?* Reaching up with his right hand, he ran his fingers through his hair trying to get a better look.

At that very moment, he noticed a gold-colored band wrapped around his middle finger. He pulled his hand down and quickly inspected it. It was a ring, a brilliant gold ring with unusual writings and curious shapes of all different sizes engraved into the precious metal, though Kristoff could not make out any familiar text. Two engravings particularly stood out to Kristoff. First, a horizontal slender figure eight with a tiny round emerald recessed into the openings of the circles in the figure eight. The second engraving was to the right of the figure eight and with one equally sized round ruby embedded in the center of an engraved sun. The engravings reminded Kristoff of symbols he had often seen in pictures associated with Egyptian artifacts.

Kristoff grabbed the ring and pulled it off his finger. Immediately he felt ill and weak, and a general sense of malaise blanketed his entire body. He promptly slid the ring back on his finger, and his symptoms resolved as quickly as they appeared. Kristoff repeated this same process several times to ensure he wasn't imagining the entire thing. Each and every time yielded the same results. *Somehow this fancy looking medical device wrapped around my middle finger controls my health,* he deduced.

Kristoff could see in the distance what looked to be a doctor making his way down the corridor towards his direction. Kristoff lowered his hands to his sides and awaited the physician's arrival. The sizable man approached the bed cautiously and stood over Kristoff, although he didn't say a word. He stood anchored to the floor, stroking his snow-white beard between his first three fingers of his right hand, visually inspecting Kristoff from head to toe. Kristoff peeked through the slits in his eyelids to catch a better glimpse of his onlooker. The rather plump man's dark weathered face was a stark contrast to the white surgical cap crowning his frosty mane, and the soft white beard that covered half of his face. Deep crevassed wrinkles in his leathery cheeks and crow's feet seemed to tell endless stories of adventure, filled with danger and excitement. Today's choice of wardrobe was a medical gown so snug at the stomach it looked as if he was smuggling in a beach ball under his surgical smock. A gut feeling told Kristoff that this was not a doctor at all. This man was up to something, and he wanted to know what it was.

"I've never seen a doctor with a big moppy beard before." Kristoff's eyes were now wide open looking up at the stranger at his bedside.

"You can see me?" the chubby man whispered.

"Yes, of course I can see you," Kristoff replied. "You're kinda hard not to miss, given your size and all."

The large man stood frozen where he stood and stroked his whiskers once again. "Kristoff, I've been checking on you every hour since you arrived. You have been completely unconscious, which is a common reaction that occurs when the ring is first placed on a new hand. The same healing process and transformation came to me when the ring was placed on my right hand all those years ago."

Kristoff gave a curious look. "I beg your pardon, sir, but did you say 'transformation years ago and having the ring placed on your own hand'?"

The tubby man peered down at the distinct tan line on his middle finger, where a ring had once resided. He tenderly rubbed the vacant white area with his left thumb and index finger, then looked back at Kristoff.

"Yes, that ring on your hand once belonged to me. However, once I willfully removed it from my finger and placed it upon your lifeless hand, it became part of you. The gift of this ring is now infused into your soul, preserving life, and unlocking powers and magic for you to discover."

Kristoff lay deathly still and pondered what the man had told him.

He inspected the ring once more and thought more intently. Craning his head to the left, he looked up at the man. "Nonsense! This is all nonsense. You clearly sustained a head wound yourself. You should be lying in a bed receiving care of your own."

Just then, Nurse Vogel walked into the recovery room and began to approach his bedside cautiously. "Nik, you're awake! *Wunderbar*! How splendid. I have been caring for you since you arrived. I have some questions for you once you have more strength." Nurse Vogel grabbed Kristoff by the hand and palpated the pulse in his wrist. "Let me just check your heart rate, soldat. Please hold still." Kristoff closed his eyes and relaxed. "Nik, I heard you talking just now…."

"Why do you keep calling me, Nik?" Kristoff interrupted.

"Well, that is your name, isn't it, soldat? It was on your name tag when they brought you in. As I was saying before you interrupted me, I heard you talking to someone when I entered the room a few moments ago. I'm curious, soldat, who were you speaking to?"

Kristoff's eyes popped open, and he looked over at the man standing behind her. "I'm talking to the man standing behind you. He came in before you did, tell me all sorts of nonsense regarding this ring on my hand."

Nurse Vogel lowered Kristoff's hand back to the bed and looked behind her. "What man are you referring to?"

Frustrated, Kristoff raised his voice. "Clearly, the only other man in the room. The white-haired man standing behind you."

"She can't see me or hear me. All she can see or hear are the two of you in this recovery room." The elderly man looked firm in his words and made no further attempt to convince Kristoff.

"You're telling me, nurse, that you just didn't hear him speak and you can't see him either? Ah, you're in on this as well, aren't you? Pulling one over on the wounded guy, I see."

The nurse left the bedside and scribbled some notes on the clipboard assigned to his medical bed, then departed the room.

What was on that clipboard? What did she write down? He couldn't resist. He had to find out. Kristoff got to his feet and hobbled over to the table where she left the clipboard. There in hurried handwriting he could make out a medical order.

"(Psych. eval and treatment for suspected head trauma. Of note, the patient is speaking to an unseen individual in the room, possible hallucinations, and possible amnesia. Doesn't recall his name being Nik)."

Kristoff returned back to his bed and quietly lay back down, feeling slightly numb inside. He closed his eyes, hoping to make this all go away. His self-diagnosed euphoria was more convincing when a voice reached his ears from the left side of his bed.

"As I said Kristoff, she neither sees me nor hears me, yet here I am."

Kristoff refused to open his eyes or acknowledge his new bedside companion. He cleared his thoughts and tried not to think. Almost a solid hour passed by while he laid in his bed motionless. Certainly, enough time had passed that his hallucination should have dispersed, came his first thought. Feeling satisfied, he opened his eyes and looked straight up at the lights shining down from the ceiling overhead. He continued to stare up and did not dare look to his left side. Fixed on the dim light bulb above his head, he allowed his peripheral view to come into focus. He appeared to be alone and after some time had passed, he felt brave enough to further inspect his solitude. Glancing to his left side, he confirmed it. No white-haired lunatic stared down at him. A sense of relief washed over him like a fresh wave on a dry beach. Kristoff drank in a long deep breath, closed his eyes, and nested his head back onto his pillow. *It was my imagination all along,* he comforted himself.

His peaceful slumber lasted but a moment. A tap on his right shoulder made the tiny hairs on the back of his neck slowly lift upward, sending

shivers down his back. "Kristoff, I'm over here on your right side now."
He wasn't alone after all.

16

(A New Purpose)

"Are you ready to learn more, Kristoff?" the old man asked cheerily.

The recovering soldier would have been okay believing all of this was the result of a head trauma. The voice and the invisible man were easy to dismiss as something mental, but the ring stuck on his finger—he couldn't dismiss it as a simple figment of his imagination.

Kristoff looked to his right, and there standing transfixed on him was the man he had seen once before. "You don't need to say anything at this moment, Kristoff," the white whiskered man said. "It will take some time to grasp what I'm telling you. Wrapping your head around this information is the first, and the most difficult step. You don't need to believe me, just hear me out. You'll know what I'm saying is true, because it will sound familiar to you, yet you'll not know why.

"First things first." The old man reached out into thin air and retrieved a stool, seemingly from nowhere. One moment it wasn't there, and the next thing Kristoff knew, the old man had grabbed a four-legged wooden stool and sat comfortably on it next to Kristoff's bed. The wooden legs of the stool had been beautifully carved from oak and artfully mastered to mimic the legs of a deer. It narrowed at the distal end of each leg with a sudden enlargement, sloping outwardly to form a hoof of polished ebony. The darkened leather seat was well worn and had been hand-tooled with unusual writings, shapes, and text, similar to the ones engraved on the ring around Kristoff's finger.

"Let me introduce myself. My birth name was Corbett Hayes. I was born on the twenty-first of September 1839 in New York. I served in the Civil War as a young man commanding troops into victory when I was just twenty-two years old. My hands were also involved in some of the miraculous events during the Great War as a seasoned old man. Now, here I am just barely over the century mark in WWII. Frankly, I'm tired of war, Kristoff. But to this end, we have been called to this work, giving hope to those who have lost everything."

Kristoff remained silent, though attentive to the mysterious man. He wanted to see what further nonsense his traumatic hallucination would provide.

"Stop me if I go too fast for you," the old man said.

By this point, Kristoff was still trying to discern fact from fiction. He could not possibly believe the outlandish story he was hearing, and he wasn't even sure it was coming from a real person or a figment of his imagination. The part he found hardest to explain was how the nurse did not see the man by his side and believed that Kristoff was talking to himself. Kristoff could hear the old man rambling on next to him, yet did not pay attention to what was being said. He was trying to figure a way to prove to himself if this was real or the beginnings of insanity. *Maybe I've finally snapped,* he told himself. The thing was, he didn't feel out of control in his thoughts, and everything felt real to him. *Schizophrenia, that's it. It's just now manifesting,* he convinced himself. Kristoff now felt lower than ever with his self-diagnosis.

The noise of his recovery room invader continued on for a while, then stopped. Kristoff listened more intently with his eyes securely shut.

"You haven't been listening to me and you think you've lost your mind, don't you?" The old man's voice was now more stern. "You're trying to find a way to prove me true or rule me out as brain trauma."

Kristoff didn't say a word, but his mind filled with more frustration. He thought, *Just go away.* Silence again filled the room and then the man continued.

"I will not go away, and yes, I just read your mind. A useful gift indeed I have, if used at appropriate times, that is."

Kristoff looked to his right side and for the first time in what seemed like hours, opened his eyes.

"You want proof, do you, young man? Well, sometimes seeing is believing after all."

The elderly man stood up, and in the same fashion as before, reached into thin air to retrieve an unseen object. Astonishingly, the man pulled his hand back firmly grasping the rim of a military helmet and placed it on the foot of Kristoff's bed.

"That's your solution? Putting a Stahlhelm on the foot of my bed?" Kristoff asked. "How, may I ask, does that prove you are not imaginary?"

Mr. Hayes sat back on his stool and did not respond to Kristoff's inquiry. The two men stared blankly at the helmet, sharing the space on Kristoff's bed. Nurse Vogel entered the room in a hurried march, pushing a medical cart with squeaky wheels. Her eyes were fixed straight ahead as she transported medical supplies to the back of the room. The clamoring wheels came to a halt, and within seconds the stern woman stood in dismay at the foot of Kristoff's bed, completely unaware of Mr. Hayes's existence.

"So, an unauthorized visitor came to visit you while I was away, no?" The nurse pursed her lips and closely inspected the helmet, tilting it in various angles, trying to catch the best light from overhead. "The Dummkopf left in such a hurry, he forgot to take his Stahlhelm with him. Leaving his helmet behind may very well be the death of him, in one way or another." As quick as she appeared, she was gone, toting the helmet out of the room.

Stunned, Kristoff laid motionless. Everything he had grown up believing and observing in life was now in question and challenged. Magic, miracles, things from bedtime stories—all were now on the table for consideration.

What is true, what is real, what is life really all about? he thought.

One after another the questions kept flooding his mind. Kristoff felt rattled and needed time to process it all, and the old man knew it. Unknown to Kristoff, Mr. Hayes instantly disappeared, leaving the recovering soldier alone to ponder. Kristoff was becoming aware that life appeared to have a more significant purpose, a higher meaning, something greater than he could currently understand. He now felt that there might be forces around him that made the world work, powers that he didn't know existed, and a greater plan for the human race. Things taught out of the Bible to him by his mother seemed to be less plausible and now factual.

The evening sun melted away as usual that night, and the sun's early rays warmed the room the next morning. Day after day this same event repeated itself while Kristoff became stronger, and his health improved. He was no longer talking to an invisible man, and the numerous consulting physicians that had visited him during the past few days dismissed the nurse's prior diagnosis and ruled him fit for service in the Führer's army once again. Five days had passed since his world had been shaken by things he couldn't understand. Many new wounded soldiers had been brought to the medical wing, and the nurses had been doing their best to keep up. Additional nurses came and went, and the room was in constant motion. Mr. Hayes had not returned since his mysterious departure, and Kristoff began to wonder why, or even if he would ever see him again.

The only good news Kristoff had received to date was that the wounds on his body had miraculously healed, and he was now awaiting discharge orders from the hospital as well as reassignment back to his military unit. The minutes stretched into hours. Finally on the seventh day since his life changing events, Kristoff had been reassigned. Nurse Vogel informed Kristoff that an officer was waiting in a private room to discuss his orders and requested that he follow her. Kristoff had been supplied with a new military-issued uniform with new boots that he had fasted tightly around his ankles. Curiously, his uniform had no identification or ranking on it. He also had not been given a new erkennungsmarke yet. His old dog tag had been removed once he arrived at the hospital.

Through the doorway and down the dim lit hall, Kristoff followed behind the nurse. A windowless door on the right side of the hall with the word "**PRIVAT**" in black lettering is where they stopped. Nurse Vogel gently knocked on the door, cracking it open slightly.

"The soldier is here to see you now sir."

"Sehr gut, send him in," said a voice from inside the room.

Kristoff pushed the door open wider and walked in. He quickly scanned the office, noting that the lamp on the desk was the only light source in the room. It supplied a dim yellow glow that brushed the walls and cast shadows in all directions. The office was a simple one and lacked decor of any sort. No pictures, flags, or personal items were evident in the room. If not for a desk and two chairs, one which was occupied with the officer, the room would be completely empty.

Kristoff closed the door behind him and slid into the wooden armchair facing the desk. The officer behind the desk was sifting through the paperwork in the lower drawer. The man's large rounded back is all that Kristoff could make out as the man continued his earnest search.

"Ah-ha …. here it is, found it at last." The officer straightened up, allowing the dismal lamp to illuminate his face. At that moment, the two men locked eyes across the desk from one another. Kristoff's eyes widened as he stared in disbelief.

17

Magical Breath of Life

"Everything has been, drunter und drüber, topsy turvy, since I arrived at this hospital," Kristoff vented. Everything that he had once considered abnormal or even paranormal was now fitting snugly into the normal category.

"Please sit down, Kristoff," the man behind the desk said. "I'm sure you were not expecting to see me, were you?" The large man chuckled, relishing Kristoff's surprised expression. "You should have seen your expression, Kristoff. From my standpoint, it truly was humorous." The air in the room lifted a little, even though it was at Kristoff's expense.

"Okay, you have my undivided attention, sir." Kristoff sat heavier in his chair. "Mr. Hayes, I cannot understand everything that has happened up to this very moment. For the past five days, I have come to believe or better yet, convince myself that I had some sort of head trauma, given my new white hair and this scar on my right cheek. You know, I didn't notice the scar on my face the first time I saw my reflection. I had been so preoccupied by my new snow-topped head that it wasn't until I looked into a real mirror that additional battle injuries emerged. I no longer believe you are or were a figment of my imagination. I can see

130

this is all very real. I just can't explain to you—the white hair, the scar, the nurse not seeing you. I can't explain anything anymore. Tell me, what can you explain about my unusual condition, Mr. Hayes? Can you help fill in the blanks?"

Mr. Hays stroked his beard gently and stared at Kristoff just like he did the first time he entered the medical wing. "Yes, I have many details to explain to you, many answers to provide you. I can explain everything to you, I can enlighten your mind and help ease the burdening questions that are weighing you down. You see, Kristoff, it was necessary to go through the past several difficult days in order for you to open your mind, humble yourself and allow me to prepare your mind to comprehend what I am going to share with you. Honestly, what I will share with you is not an easy thing to believe in. Specifically for you, it would have almost been impossible to believe had you not gone through a sort of purging of previous beliefs. The unbelieving are often the most difficult to convince without a major manifestation of unexplained events."

Pushing his chair back from the desk Mr. Hays leaned back in his chair and continued. "I have known about you for a while. You see, I also was injured in war, a Civil war in the United States. My life was preserved after a fatal injury during that war. On that occasion, when I awoke, I had on that very ring that is fixed to your hand. The gentleman that placed that ring on my hand, eventually explained to me that he had been observing me for a while as well. This ring preserved my life and prepared me to take over once my predecessor's time was completed here on earth, giving me time to learn of my duties and abilities pronounced upon me." He later told me that he had been instructed through impressions that entered his mind that I would be the one to eventually take over for him.

Mr. Hays stood up and walked around his desk and sat on the front corner of the desk. "Kristoff, each individual selected may be called for any given amount of time, at least until his mission on the earth has been completed and the next individual is ready to take over. It has been said that some of our forebears have spent a few centuries in the mission before being relieved from their assignment. Each time a replacement comes, the predecessor has impressions and is guided to the location of his replacement. Once on location, he is to observe them unseen until the moment of the required selfless act of love of giving their life for another has arrived.

"You said you have been observing me, what do you mean?' asked Kristoff. "As I said earlier, I have been watching you for a while now. I was with you that terrible night when you rescued Lorelei from the fire, that time you wanted to stand up to the Nazis' while they ravaged towns and Jewish communities. I walked with you during the final moments of your life. I knew Gunter was in the trees behind you in the wooded area that surrounded the house. He watched you like a tiger observing his prey. He was alone and talked to himself quietly about how he was going to be the hero by killing that family. I watched him selfishly gun you down in a fit of rage and pride. After he abandoned your corpse and scurried away, I rushed to your side, removed my ring, and placed it on your hand. The magical breath of life entered your lungs once again, and the wounds began to heal. It was at that moment for us that the passing of the torch began.

Kristoff looked down at the ring that had been placed on his hand, took in a long deep breath in and slowly let it.

"Kristoff, I carried you unseen to the hospital where I knew you could get care and recovery. I have… just as you now have, the ability to walk unseen to onlookers. This will all take time to develop and learn. The transformation phase started the moment I removed the ring from my hand and placed it on your finger Kristoff. For some individuals the transformation begins slowly and yet for others, fairly quickly. The process of your transformation has been quicker than it was for me all those years ago. For example, look how quickly I became visible to you, when others could not see me, unless permitted. This is why I was a little surprised when you saw me that first day. I didn't realize the transformation taking place was so rapid for you. As you grow stronger in your abilities, I will grow weaker until it is time for me to be called home at last. The time for Margret and me to rest is soon at hand.

"Margret?" Kristoff butted in with an inquisitive look.

"Yes, I have my dear Margaret by my side. You have someone special too Kristoff. Mr. Hays stood up, straightened his back, and pointed his finger at Kristoff. "Make sure you protect her and help her to fulfill her mission here with you." Kristoff nodded his head. "I will sir. I promised a long time ago to always look after her. She is the world to me."

Mr. Hays flashed a satisfied grin at Kristoff. "Let me share a few things of significant importance with you. That ring on your hand. It cannot be removed by others. It can only be removed by you, by your own free will and with the knowledge you surrender yourself to the rules of mortality once again allowing death to claim your tabernacle of clay. This ring has been passed down from one person to the next since it's divine reception. The ring is who we are, the source of the magic which creates the miracles. Many things regarding the ring are still a mystery, Kristoff. The thing that is clear, is that magic of the ring only works for the good of others and for selfless causes. Power from the ring cannot be controlled for selfish gain, or earthly praise from man. Each attempt will only weaken the ring's magical ability, until the power to sustain our life will all but fade away, leaving none to continue the cause.

"What is that?" asked Kristoff.

"The cause to help others to remember that there is a true and living God. We are His children and He loves us. Each act of kindness or miracle performed helps promote hope, love, and even sparks a belief that there is an almighty God. It helps people feel that we are truly not alone, and that we are known to Him. Your mission is to continue to help reduce pain, restore hope, help others to remember in deity, a divine God, his loving Son. This is our mission. This is now your mission. Kristoff, you are to share love and help promote hope.

"During Christmas, Santa is remembered and then forgotten for a season. I fear that the same can be said about our Savior, whose birth we are remembering. Our focus is and always will be to help others remember Christ, his divine role and superior love for us. One way we can do this is to help spread love, hope, and kindness abroad. Have you ever noticed, Kristoff, that the world is a little kinder, more giving and more patient during the Christmas season. Let's do our part to help others feel that same gift of charity every day of the year.

"Kristoff, please reach into your shirt pocket and remove the half-moon spectacles in your pocket."

Kristoff followed the instructions perfectly like a student on the first day of school.

"Please put them on, and let me know what you see."

The glasses were made of brass and flexed comfortably at the hinges. The half-moon glass appeared very old and the lenses were not as transparent or clear as today's ocular aids. Kristoff opened the arms of spectacles and propped them gently on the bridge of his nose. Swirling vapors of red and green smoke appeared in the foggy glass the moment the brass touched his skin. The vibrant smoke startled Kristoff at first, but he did not yield to the fear or remove them. Curiosity of the animated event unfolding before his eyes drew him in even closer.

"What do you see Kristoff?" asked Mr. Hayes.

"Well….I see someone in the distance, a figure walking toward me. I can't make out who it is. It's a grayish shadow, but it feels familiar to me."

"Keep looking, Kristoff. The ability to see more clearly will develop as you learn to discern and develop your skills."

Kristoff focused more. "Mr. Hayes, I'm starting to feel scared, sad, and lonely."

"That's good, Kristoff. You're starting to feel the emotions of the person you're seeing. You're making contact with the emotional feeling created by what you are seeing."

The images cleared and were more distinguishable every passing second. The sad figure in his view turned its head and looked directly at Kristoff. "It's Lorelei!" Kristoff shouted. "What am I looking at? What is this? What does this mean?"

The old man looked over at Kristoff. "These are visionary glasses, Kristoff. They can see the present, past, and sometimes the future. You see, we have been given the ability to see things that are unseen to others, yet it does have its limits. The glasses can sense our needs and desires. In time you'll be able to use them for good and to control what you are able to see. These glasses have proven to be very useful when looking for history locks to help time travel. History locks have been created

"So, was this a vision of the future, past, or present of Lorelei?" Kristoff asked, anxiously.

"I find it useful to pay close attention to detail when using the glasses at first. Details can provide help in many circumstances," Mr. Hayes said. "In time you'll be able to discern the meaning of what you see or desire to see. Look at the surroundings, the lighting. Is it dark, is there a sunset, a clock, or certain vegetation in bloom? This helps determine the time frame. Background images can help with locations."

Kristoff reached up, yanking the spectacles off in one sweeping motion. "Here, you take them Mr. Hayes. You put them on, find Lorelei, and tell me what's going on!" Kristoff demanded.

"I'm afraid it doesn't work that way, Kristoff. You only discover what your heart is desiring to see. This vision is unique for you. Besides, I passed these on to you. They belong to you now and cannot be loaned out."

"What if someone besides me looks through them, or what if I misplace them and can't find them?"

"First, anyone that looks through them will only see what regular glasses would see. It will appear as a normal pair of spectacles. As for losing them, don't worry. You must understand that the ring and the glasses go together. If for some reason you misplace your glasses, simply look in your pocket once again and you'll find them. They will always reappear when you need them. They left my pocket the instant I put the ring on your finger. The curious thing about Guinevere… I mean to say, the glasses have a sassy personality."

"What do you mean?" asked Kristoff.

"Oh, you'll see. Just remember, don't hesitate a second to talk to the glasses out loud and ask what you need to see. They're loyal to you and will always yield an answer, though it may come as a sassy answer, but nonetheless the answer will come. I'm going to miss Guinevere. Oh, one more thing about Guinevere, she will help you find the time traveling portals known as history locks. History locks are created through events in life associated with deep emotion that becomes locked in time. History locks are all around us Kristoff, but keep in mind that it is near impossible to find them without the use of Guinevere, though I have been lucky to stumble across a few in the past all on my own."

"Can I travel to the future through the use of the portal?" questioned Kristoff.

"No, only back in time," Mr. Hayes said. "The future hasn't happened yet. The future is always changing depending on the decisions we make. We can travel back in time in these special portals, and when we do, we're unseen to others unless we choose to be seen. Time travel is a tricky thing, and I believe this is one of the reasons we must be careful. The events that have taken place in the past have set the future, or the present time we live in. Our agency on earth permits us to act accordingly to our own desires and ultimately, we will need to stand and be judged for our actions. We're unable to change actions or events caused by others. Yes, we can time travel, but mostly for observation. However, one great feature that was discovered several generations ago is that we can travel with items we take with us from the present to the past, but we can't take things from the past to our time. In addition, only items that were in existence in the period of time that we travel to will travel with us. Essentially, I believe we are prevented from introducing technology before it's appropriate time. Time travel is the key to Christmas. This may help explain to you how Santa can be in so many places in such an impossible amount of time.

"You have no doubt noticed my physical appearance and that yours has been changing. First off, let me share that Santa hasn't always looked this way. Our physical appearance is conditional on what people believe we should look like. If the world wanted to believe we were skinny or muscular, this is the form we take on. In earlier times we wore suits of blue, green, and even a dim yellow coat. If I recall correctly, it wasn't until somewhere around the 1860s that people started to believe we should be wearing a red suit. Since that time, our apparel and our physical form have taken on different shapes, specifically around the middle, so to say."

His chuckling comment made his belly jiggle in delight.

"Your hair was the first thing to change. Don't worry, you'll hold your physical physique for a while still, Kristoff. The hair changes to white in all of us. It is a reaction that happens when the magic of the ring preserves your life and flows through your veins. It is evidence of magic and your immortality. You will continue to grow into your elder years and then the aging process yields to magic. You will remain at that age until the time of your mission is completed, or the world decides to believe you should look differently. Given the history, I don't see that Santa will look much different."

Kristoff softly traced the scar on his right cheek. "What can you tell me about this? I distinctly remember I did not have a scar on my face before."

"Each and every Santa has that exact scar. Here look." Mr. Hayes unbuttoned his long sleeve shirt and revealed an identical scar on his left forearm. "I tell the curious that it was from a farming accident as a child. It appeared when the ring was placed on my hand during the first Great War. Unfortunately, we don't pick the location of the scar. For you, sadly it is on your face. However, this works out in your favor. Think of it as a ….sort of disguise. With your white hair and scar, most will never recognize you. I took the liberty of changing your name on military records using your middle name to be your first and modifying your last name. I thought it was very fitting, giving you are Santa. You are now Nik Kringle. I took the liberty of changing your dog tag the day I brought you to the hospital. You can always go back to Kristoff when this terrible war ends. Until then, we have created you an alias, and you'll be returning to the fight. Your mission is just beginning, Nik. You need you to get back into the war. Your passion to save others and protect the Jews is needed. Remember, you're immortal, though you can be wounded, feel pain, and fear. You'll not die, and if you do receive wounds, you'll recover. You're in control of how you manage your responsibilities. You'll learn and develop your skills in time. Our paths will not likely cross again. I'm finishing my mission and you're starting yours. Go, Nik, get back out there. You need to find Lorelei. Never reveal your secret, but to those in whom you can trust."

Nik stood, turned, and headed for the door. Stopping in his tracks he blurted out, "What about Christmas, kids, and gifts?"

"The miracle of all miracles, Nik, is that Christmas will still happen. It's not about the gifts at all. It's the love of Christ and the remembrance of His birth. Mortal men help continue the magic of Christmas and you'll know what miracles to help with through inspiration. You'll know your role in all of this soon enough."

Nik turned around to further question Mr. Hayes but found himself alone in the room.

18

The March to Dieppe

The front brakes shrilled in objection as the massive transport truck came to a halt. "Verschwinde! Verschwinde!" the seated driver commanded while slapping his hand against his door. Without delay, the battle-ready soldiers jumped off the back of the mud-splattered truck and gathered under the camouflage of the nearby bocage. Over a half a year had passed since Gunter had taken Kristoff's life in a rage of pride. Gunter, a polished fabricator of stories, had returned to his post following his assault on Kristoff and loudly publicized that Die Eule was in fact Kristoff. And when he had confronted Kristoff about this while on secret assignment, Kristoff admitted to it, and in order to conceal his secret, he had attempted to kill Gunter. Gunter's story described how he was able to overpower Kristoff and outwit him. Ultimately, as the story had been repeatedly shared, Kristoff resorted to pulling his gun, but was not a match to the superior soldier, and Gunter won the fight. He won praise from his commander Oberführer Berndt and was given special privileges, advancement in rank, and received a large increase in his monthly wages.

Kristoff's name had been dragged through the deceitful mud for more than six months and had been recorded on official military record as killed in action. As far as anyone knew, Kristoff Christkindl was a casualty of war. This was a troubling time for his friend Eckerd, who was currently stationed back in Berlin. Eckerd was serving a leader and military against his own beliefs and convictions. He knew if he did not serve, he would forfeit his own life and the lives of his family. His only comfort in this terrible war is that he was able to share his same beliefs with Kristof. With the news of his friend and confidant being killed in action, Eckerd was left alone unsure how to escape the clasp of war and the battle of justice in his own head.

Reports of heavy damage from Allied bombing of Berlin spread feverishly from soldier to soldier. Most notably in the minds of the men was the destruction of <u>Deutsche Opernhaus</u> in the <u>Berlin</u> district of <u>Charlottenburg</u>. The opera house had been destroyed by a Royal Air force air raid. The loss of that iconic building weighed heavy on the minds of the men huddled together awaiting instructions from their commanding officer.

"Heavy bombing of Berlin continues as this month of November is coming to a close, my dear soldaten," thundered the heavily cloaked officer. "Winter is pressing firmly upon us, but don't let the freezing temperatures or the recent damages of Berlin dishearten you. We are strong, and we will win this war. Germany will be victorious in the end!" The commanding officer stood only 5 feet 8 inches tall, but his confidence reached the heights of the towering beech trees. "We have been ordered to mobilize our forces along the northern French coast in preparation to defend against the anticipated Allied invasion. Soldaten, we will be heading towards Normandy on foot from here, but we'll be stationed in Dieppe for the time being. Temporary shelters in Dieppe have been set up to receive us and additional troops over the next several months will be sent to help us fortify Normandie. The Führer insists that we make this a stronghold and dig in deep. We cannot afford to let this area fall into the hands of the Allies. Let's move out."

The commander climbed aboard his armored truck and sat close to the driver. With the forward wave of his hand, the driver pushed on the gas, and the tall knobby tires gripped the sticky wet dirt, pulling the vehicle forward. In unison, the soldiers marched behind the smoky truck, trekking their way to Dieppe. "At this pace," shouted the commander, "we will be in Dieppe by nightfall!"

It was a very cold November, and with Christmas right around the corner, Kristoff questioned if the war would ever be over. His life as he now knew it was so different, from even just last year. Now here he was, marching in the cold damp mud, not knowing the location of Lorelei, or his mother, or his closest friends. Here he was alone using the alias of Nik Kringle. For Kristoff, it was all he could do to keep it together and remain positive and hopeful for the future.

The long march in the wintery mud proved to be difficult yet rewarding. Kristoff took advantage of the time ruminating for ways to help the war victims. The imagery of a yellow star of David sewn to Jews' clothing motivated Kristoff to plan some way to provide assistance to them. Many had been starved, treated poorly, and labeled as less than human under the hands of the German army. The suffering needed to end.

Throughout Kristoff's military service, he had seen various forms of the yellow star in the many regions he had been to, all labeling the individual wearing it. *I must find a way to let Jews know that I am someone that can provide help and not to fear me, but how?* As if by magic itself, an idea came together in Kristoff's mind. A red coat should be worn, something completely different than a Nazi uniform, came the impression. *Besides, with a red coat I may look like a Santa visiting a family, and if anyone was to see me, they would likely believe the family is Christian, not Jewish. This will undoubtedly also help the family stay out of focus and in secure hiding,* he thought to himself. *But where can I find red material to use, especially in a war?* Kristoff continued marching in cadence with the soldiers for the next hour, all the while racking his brain trying to think of where he could obtain red cloth to line his coat.

Finally, the solution appeared in the form of the two small red Nazi flags attached to the commanding officer whipping in the driving breeze. *I can use the flags. I can gather up the old, damaged Nazi flags I find and cut them into strips of red cloth. I can then sew the red strips of material to the inner lining of my long winter coat. If I'm ever questioned about the red coat lining, I can claim it is for increased warmth against the bitter cold.*

Later, in the dark of night, when I deliver supplies to the Jews in their hideouts, I will reverse my coat to create a red signal of safety. It won't take very long for word to spread rampantly amongst the Jews, that the man in the red coat is someone they can trust. But how will I know where to go or what house to enter? he thought. *I need some sort of secret signal to tell me where I need to go, and what house is in need.*

Without warning, a shout from the front of the line came. "Zug Halt!" the commander holding his hand high in the air.

Standing still, Kristoff felt his feet throbbing inside his tight boots. The soldiers had been marching for three hours nonstop, and Kristoff was certain he could feel three or four blisters forming.

"Kurze pause. Steig aus dem Straße!" came the next command. The order to get off the road and take a break was welcoming words to Kristoff and his aching feet.

Kristoff hustled off of the road and rested himself on a tree stump near the roadside. In an instant his right boot and sock had been removed unveiling several tender protrusions on his big toe and the back of his heel. "As I suspected," he grumbled under his breath, "blisters."

Drawing his knife from his sheath, he pierced the lesion with the tip of the blade releasing pressure and allowing the watery substance to dribble down his toe and heel. *That should help,* he thought.

After dressing the wound, he replaced his woolen sock and laced his boot snugly. With his foot and toes in better condition, Kristoff sat comfortably sipping his water and taking in a bit of the beautiful landscape that surrounded him. The vibrant green pine needles against the muddy background quickly caught Kristoff's eye. A nearby sapling Scots pine had managed to push its way through the soil, and though only eight inches tall, it seemed to stand boldly in its place, unaware of the conflict of war all around it. *That's it*, he felt assured inside. *That will be my secret signal for the man in the red coat. What I will need to do is spread the message that if help is needed, they need to place a small sapling Scots pine branch in the window and help will soon be on its way.*

"Die Pausenzeit ist vorbei."

His strategic planning was disrupted when the commander ended the break time. The fatigued soldiers pried their over-marched bodies from their resting places and once again found themselves in line walking on the road through the countryside. For reasons unknown to Kristoff, the hike was not so daunting this time. Perhaps it was because of his doctored foot, or perhaps, and better yet, because of his renewed hope to help others that lightened his spirits and put a new pip in his step.

During the lengthy march, Kristoff found himself surveying the area and scouting for an area to return to in the night. Small farmhouses dotted the tree line in the distance as they walked the backroads towards Dieppe. His plan to help others was admirable. However, the reality of how difficult this was going to be to find the hiding Jewish families started to sink in.

Here I am, Santa, with powers to bring happiness and restore hope, but I can't even find the people to help. What good is my ability if I can't even use it? he questioned himself. Kristoff found himself reflecting on the conversation he had with Mr. Hayes in the hospital wing so long ago. That Santa had shared with him the ability to see things unseen but needed. Kristoff remembered that if he ever needed Guinevere the glasses, they would appear for him. "When we get to Dieppe tonight, I'll try to find Guinevere and see if by using them, I can find a family to help. If I can find someone, I'll then use the glasses to locate a time travel portal to take me there."

Kristoff was now both excited and anxious. This would be the night that Kristoff would be using his magic for the first time by himself. The thought of using magic was thrilling yet made him a little nervous, since anything could go wrong. After all, he was a rookie in the magic department, and this was basically on the job training. "We learn from our mistakes," he reassured himself. He could always find comfort in his mother's words of advice.

The long march came to a dog-weary end just as the evening sun melted in the distant horizon. A temporary camp in Dieppe had been set up to receive the incoming troops, and by the looks of things, it had been here for quite some time. The camp was well occupied and quite busy when the men arrived. Military officers were seen walking together in a hurried manner and would suddenly duck into a staff tent and out of sight. Charcoal gray puffs of smoke could be seen emanating from the wood burning stove pipes, blanketing the entire makeshift camp with smells of burning wood. Some soldiers had found warmth by gathering around the smoldering embers inside of an old metal barrel located near the infantry tents. Soldier and military staff tents of various sizes dotted the campsite along with armored vehicles, several cannons, 3 Panzer tanks, and several transport vehicles covered in mud could be seen being refueled and serviced by mechanics.

Upon arriving at Dieppe, the troops had been dismissed and assigned to their infantry tents. Up to this point, Kristoff, now known to others as Nik, had not taken the time to get to know the other soldiers around him. Some onlookers stared at his white hair and others also preferred not to speak to him. He found the silence around him therapeutic while readjusting to the war assignments. The lack of conversation helped keep him from being distracted and allowed him to gather his thoughts and develop his rescue plans for the victims of the war.

"Kringle!" his commander called out from a tent thirty yards away. "Kringle, grab your things. You'll bunk here for the unforeseen future."

Kristoff grabbed his pack, throwing it over his right shoulder, and headed toward his tent. "Find a cot inside and make it yours, Kringle. Food has been prepared, and it will still be warm if you hurry. Get a good rest tonight. Tomorrow there is much to be done."

Kristoff entered the tent, finding himself alone. Twelve military cots filled the tent, arranged in four rows with three cots to a row, all end to end. Military packs had been left on the tops of all the cots. However, three remained vacant. Kristoff spotted two open cots near the back of the tent and chose one of them for his temporary residence.

Outside the tent, the commander continued ordering additional soldiers to report to their assigned tents. "Schmidt, Krause, you'll bunk here. Fichtmann, Bartels, you'll be bunking here. Grab your things, sich beeilen. Get a move on!" Heavy footsteps could be heard coming toward the tent. Kristoff dropped his pack to the floor, shoving it under his cot. The tent door flung open, and two winded soldiers stumbled inside. "I'll take this one," a short stocky soldier exclaimed, sitting down on a cot close to Kristoff.

"Right then, I'll take the last one over in the corner," the other replied.

Kristoff hunched forward on his cot with his eyes closed. He rubbed his thumbs on the temples of his head.

"Hallo Mitbewohner, we are roommates." The stocky stubby nosed soldier said to Kristoff as he tossed his pack onto the open cot. "Kringle, I heard the commander call you. I have heard of your name before. Let me think…oh, yes, I remember now. Kris must be your first name, or do they just call you Santa?"

Kristoff's face was now buried deep in his hands, massaging his forehead with his fingertips. "Nein," he said, and he shook his white-haired head in protest. "I go by Nik."

"Nice to meet you, Nik. We're heading for some grub. You want to join us?"

Kristoff shook his head again. "Thanks, but no. I'm going to rest a bit. Perhaps call it an early evening."

"I understand, Nik. Been there myself. I'll bring ya something back from the kitchen. My name is Fitchmann, by the way," he said while walking to the tent door. "But my friends call me Eckerd." Kristoff looked up just in time to see the soldier slip through the doorway and out of sight.

19

E.L.F.

The chattering of soldiers could be heard as Kristoff sat on the edge of his bed staring at the doorway, trying to wrap his head around what he had just heard.

I thought the voice sounded familiar. This is great! Eckerd has no idea who his new bunkmate is. My hands must have hid my face, Kristoff thought. Thrilled that they were to be reunited, he began to plot out his surprise reveal to Eckerd. He was excited to surprise him, yet careful not to draw attention. If Eckerd was to recognize him right away, he may shout out in excitement which could compromise Kristoff's true identity. Kristoff had to be discreet.

An hour had passed since Kristoff had watched his friend disappear through the tent door. The excitement of the reunion mixed with some anxiety was enough to cause his innards to tumble around. Each passing minute felt like forever as he lay in his bunk. Kristoff faced the tent wall and covered himself with his blanket. For anyone entering the tent, it would appear that he had retired for the evening. Kristoff listened intently for any movement of the tent.

At last, the anticipated shuffling of boots entering the tent were heard.

Several soldiers began to enter the tent in groups of two or three, each being careful not to disturb their sleeping comrade. Kristoff heard the creaking beds as the men sat slowly and began to remove their boots. Whispers and ongoing conversions in a hushed tone filled the room.

"Hey look, Kringle is exhausted. Sound asleep already that guy," Eckerd spoke softly to no one in particular. Quietly, Eckerd slipped out of his boots and uniformed shirt. Reaching down to his bed, he pulled back his woolen blanket to crawl in for the night.

"What is that?" Eckerd asked.

Exposed by the removal of the blanket was an eight-inch length of braided blond hair that had been tied together by a strap of torn material serving as a ribbon. Eckerd stood transfixed at the unexpected finding on his bed, trying to make sense of it. Inspecting the braid closer, he noted that it was clean, soft, and looked well cared for. This was obviously a memento, something given to a soldier to remember his sweetheart back home.

"Why is this on my bed?" His thoughts raced inside his head as he looked around the tent for an answer. Soldiers in the tent paid no attention to Eckerd and were busy settling in for the night. Eckerd hoped to make eye contact with the guilty party, but all appeared to be unaware of anything unusual going on.

Eckerd, unsure what to do with the hair and slightly embarrassed to be on the receiving end of a prank, placed the hair under his bed and out of sight. Lying on his back, he pondered the meaning of the braid and who could have placed it there. The only one in the tent while he was at dinner was the white-haired Kringle, who was sleeping like a log. Determined to get to the bottom of the mystery, Eckerd pulled the braid out from under the bed and inspected it once again. The tightened material binding the hair together looked like it could have been from a torn uniform, but Eckerd wasn't certain. A closer inspection of the material revealed inked letters with a small heart next to them: **K.C. +**

L.B.

Small hairs on the back of Eckerd's neck stood up.

"Kris Christkindl and Lorelei Blumenfeld? …. Could it possibly be Lorelei's hair?"

Eckerd cast an eye at his sleeping bunk mate, bewildered about how the white-haired man had ended up with the braided hair.

"Kringle, you awake over there?"

A muffled moan came from under the makeshift jacket Kristoff was using as a pillow to cover his head.

"I say, Kringle, how did this braided hair end up on my bunk? What gives?"

Kristoff's heart was thundering in his chest as he slowly twisted toward his friend. The jacket slipped off Kristoff's head, exposing the backside of his clean-cut white mane. Seconds later, he pivoted his body and faced his friend. Eckerd fell back on his cot, and he sat on his bed, staring open-mouthed at Kristoff.

"Shut your mouth before a bug crawls in it," Kristoff said.

Eckerd slowly closed his mouth, and his eyes darted from Kristoff's white hair, then to the scar, back to his hair, then to his eyes. "I know those eyes of yours, but your hair and scar conflict with what I know," Eckerd said.

A grin stretched across Kristoff's face. "Your suspicion is correct, Eckerd. It's me, Kristoff." The next thing Kristoff knew, Eckerd had leaped from his bed and was squeezing the breath out of Kristoff with the biggest hug.

"I thought you were dead Kristoff," Eckerd whispered, gipping his friend harder.

"Eckerd, I can't breathe," moaned Kristoff.

Letting go of Kristoff, Eckerd quickly wiped tears from his eyes. "The white hair, the scar, your death. What happened, Kristoff?" Eckerd asked.

"You can't call me Kristoff anymore, at least during the war. You must call me Nik. We cannot afford to blow my cover. Come, sit down, and I'll explain."

The two stayed up the remainder of the night swapping stories and getting caught up. Kristoff explained everything to Eckerd, and to his surprise, Eckerd believed every word, although he stumbled to believe the part about Kristoff becoming Santa. It wasn't until Kristoff pulled Guinevere out of his pocket and had Eckerd try to remove the ring on his hand that Eckerd began to believe it.

"I had a hard time believing it too, but this is the truth. It took a lot to convince me as well. I saw Lorelei through these glasses. I know she's alive, but I don't know where she is. Have you heard anything?"

A curious look flashed across Eckerd's face. "You see, Kris …. Uh, Nik, I actually know exactly where she is. We've been in contact since your 'death.' I made it a mission to find Lorelei and let her know of the news. This is when I ran into Bartels."

"Who?" asked Kristoff.

You know, Dennis Bartels. The soldier I left to eat with. After your death, I was transferred to Berlin and was placed in intelligence. Apparently, the higher ups heard about my skills, and they wanted me to find individuals or groups joining the resistance and impeding the work of the Führer. Bartels worked there as well and soon enough we became friends. He had been working alone and doing what we would do, warn the Jews of raids." Eckerd scooted forward to the edge of his seat and straightened his back. "We teamed up and continued the mission you and I were doing before we were separated. We also recruited several others along the way that felt the same as us. There are about fifteen of us now going about foiling raids and executions." This war is ugly and there are some that have been forced to join. We wear the uniform by force, but we do not follow the ideology pressed on us. In some of our intelligence briefings, we heard that the Die

Eule had been eliminated. We felt they were referring to you. This is when we felt you may have been killed." Eckerd looked down at his feet, paused for a moment and continued. "When further investigating the story, we found records that you had been killed in action. I took it upon myself to locate your mother and I personally let her know of her loss. It was a very difficult day for all of us. Soon after, she moved to Denmark traveling with two families trying to escape Germany. I continued to keep correspondence with your mother for quite a while." Eckerd looked up from his feet and stared directly into Kristoff's eyes. "I see where you get your compassion for others. Elsa is just like you. She is always looking for a way to help others. In fact, she had been very helpful getting information to Jewish families of scheduled raids. She doesn't fear death or think of her own life. She cares for so many.

"Funny thing I gotta share with you. We call our secret group E.L.F. Yes, ELF. We go about doing good in secret like elves, so he thought it was appropriate. Besides It was Bartels's idea. He said to me, let's use your initials Eckerd Lambart Fichtmann. So, E.L.F it was." Eckerd smiled proudly.

"What about Lorelei?" Kristoff asked again.

"I was getting to that part. Since Bartels and I worked in intelligence and had reports to sift through, we looked for someone matching Lorelei's description and situation. We found that her name had been recorded, and more than once she had been found hiding and helping Jews in various towns. She has eluded capture, but in a raid on a home she was in, everyone fled the house so quickly that she had to leave her personal belongings behind, including her documents. This is how her identity was discovered. Since that time, she has been on the run. Fortunately for us, we have eyes on the ground in many areas. The latest intel is that she's here in Normandy. Working as nachrichtendienst does have special privileges. Since we are intelligence, we were given permission to assign ourselves to a Kompanie as a way of gathering further intel. This is why Dennis and I assigned ourselves to be here. We're not actually gathering intel; we're planning on finding Lorelei to get her out of here. It's not by coincidence that we're in the same Kompanie. Our plan was to find her and get her back with her parents."

"Her parents? You know where her parents are?"

"Yes, we do," Eckerd continued. "The Blumenfelds fled the Poland zoo to Denmark in hopes of getting to Sweden. Danes had been secretly sending their Jewish countrymen to Sweden by means of dangerous boat crossings. Lorelei's parents made it safely to Denmark, caught up with your mother, and they made it to Sweden where they now reside. We have plans to get Lorelei out of this war and back to her parents in Sweden."

A wave of relief flooded Kristoff. He stared blankly at the floor, pondering something important. His lips stretched into a grin, allowing a chuckle to slip through.

"This is so fascinating. Don't you see it? More is at play here. Our pathways have been laid out before us. I don't believe this is mere coincidence."

"What do you mean?" Eckerd asked.

"Well, here you have been part of a secret group of individuals, all with the same purpose we share. It just so happens that someone suggested that you call your group E.L.F., and I have been called to be Santa. Don't you think that is curious?"

Eckerd looked in the direction of Dennis, then back at Kristoff. "I guess we're all destined for something bigger than ourselves. Consider us all in." His outstretched hand was met by Kristoff's, and once again they vowed to help the destitute.

Kristoff and Eckerd continued talking through the night. Kristoff relished this opportunity to share his secret with someone. He felt the weight on his shoulders lighten as he continued to share the details of his new life and mission. At length, the dark night began to give way to the warm rays of the sun welcoming the new day. For a moment, the world didn't seem to be so bad. Despite staying up all night, Kristoff and Eckerd felt no fatigue. They both had been invigorated by the hopes of a better future.

The tent door flung open, pushing the cold morning air over the sleeping men.

"Edermann, antreten drausen in fünf Minuten!" a commanding voice shouted through the opening. The man was gone in an instant. However, his booming voice could be heard in the next tent repeating the same order to other sleeping soldiers.

"Well, that was a pleasant wake-up call" Bartels mumbled from the comfort of his warm bed. "All right, men!" he shouted. "You heard the man. We need to be outside and ready in five minutes. Let's get going!"

All the soldiers jumped to their feet and scrambled to get dressed.

Kristoff looked at Eckerd. "Hey, we need to pair up with Bartels at some point today. If he is one of us, we need to let him know who I am so we can start making plans." Eckerd nodded his head, and the two reunited friends exited the tent.

20

A Bag of Surprises

"Bitter morning air, this is," whispered Bartels. Kristoff and Eckerd stood in formation to the left of Bartels and had just barely made it in time to avoid punishment for being late.

"That was a close one," Eckerd whispered to Bartels.

The icy air had made moving more difficult than usual. Kristoff felt his legs quiver and wasn't sure if he was feeling a small earthquake under his feet or if it was his body shivering under protest of the brisk breeze cutting through his uniform. Gradually gentle beams of the sun highlighted the landscape of the camp and came to a rest on the field-gray double-breasted long coat of their commander standing in front of the chilled men. The dark green collar and matching shoulder straps were commonly seen on the long field jackets. However, something was different about this one. Scarlet turnback lapels and highly polished gold buttons reflecting in the sun revealed that this was an officer's coat.

"My name is Lieutenant Heydrich," the broad-shouldered man informed his platoon. The hardened officer stood a solid six feet tall. He had pressed a well-worn spectacle over his right eye. A thin chain connecting the round glass dangled over his square jawline and disappeared just below the chin. The man's weathered face and sunken eyes revealed a fatigue that had not been felt by the soldiers. "I have been in command of this camp for many months, and we have had success in our preparations for any attacks that may come to Normandy or if any—" The lieutenant stopped, pondering his next statement. "I have been informed early this morning that my replacement will arrive later this afternoon. Now, listen closely as you'll be assigned to your duties for today."

Lieutenant Heydrich began assigning groups of men from the platoon. "You six men will help other platoons to position and camouflage long-range guns overlooking the beach," he said, pointing to a group of soldiers to the right of Kristoff. "You men," he said, pointing to a group of ten, "have been assigned to help transport ammunition to bunkers, and various strongholds at the tops of cliffs."

After several more assignments, Lieutenant Heydrich addressed Bartels, Kristoff, and Eckerd. "You three men," he said, looking slightly sympathetically, "you have, unfortunately, drawn the short straw this time. I need you three to fill sandbags. You'll be sent to the beach where supplies are located and waiting. A Maultier will meet up with you later in the day to pick up your filled bags. The half-track truck will be able to haul as many bags as you can fill."

Lieutenant Heydrich pointed at Kristoff. "Kringle, you're in charge of your group. The three of you need to rotate your duties: one to fill, one to hold the bag, and the other to stack the bag. Rotation is key here in order to prevent fatigue."

Turning to the platoon, Lieutenant Heydrich continued, "You're to return here at sixteen hundred hours, where you'll form ranks once again. Your new commander will be introduced. Make the Führer proud. Dismissed!" With that command, the platoon fell out of formation and proceeded to their assigned areas.

"Make the Führer proud, eh?" jeered Bartels. "That is the last thing I want to do."

Kristoff flashed a smile at Eckerd. The three men paced themselves as they walked the half mile to the beach. The dark blue ocean water slowly melted into the distant horizon.

"You smell that, boys?" Eckerd asked the others.

"Smell what?" Bartels asked.

Kristoff drew in a long breath through his nostrils and held it briefly. "Ocean! I smell the ocean."

Instantly the cadence of their march increased as the smiling soldiers double-timed it to the sand and rolling waves. Arriving at the beach front, the men came to a sliding stop, shocked at what they were seeing. It was anything but a picnic or any previous memories the men had prior to the war. Rather than kids playing, laughter, or adults lounging, puffs of dark smoke emanated from the exhaust pipes of tractors, tanks, and trucks that dotted the beachfront. From the top of the cliffs from where the men were standing, they could see numerous soldiers darting around like busy ants on an anthill working feverishly to get their work done.

Soldiers could be seen rolling out barbed wire fence lines below them and metal barricades had been placed along the shallow waters of the shore. Large concrete bunkers with massive long metal barrels protruding were visible and placed in strategic locations.

"Anyone would be crazy to attack here," Bartels remarked. "The high ground, powerful guns, and the beach littered with blockades. It's clear to me, Hitler must need this area protected and will do anything to keep it."

"Look over there," Eckerd said, pointing to a large pile of sand at the base of the towering cliff face. Several shovels were lying on the ground. "It looks like this is the place." Eckerd led the way and was the first to grab a shovel. "I'll take the first shift on the shovel—that is, if you two don't mind."

"No problem," replied Kristoff.

"Sounds good to me," said Bartels.

The men commenced filling the bags one by one and stacked them into a pile to be transported. Perhaps it was they were now laboring or perhaps it was the slightly therapeutic motion of digging in the loose sand—regardless of the reason, once the work began, the talking came to a stop. The silence was short lived, however. Within five minutes of digging, Eckerd blurted out, "Kringle is the real Santa!"

At that declaration, the three men all came to an abrupt halt.

Bartels, who had been holding the bags being filled, straightened his back and stared blankly at Eckerd. "What was that? It sounded like you said something about Santa Claus."

"I did," replied Eckerd.

Bartels's eyebrows lowered. "I'm confused. Why are you talking about Santa while we have work to be done?"

Eckerd leaned against the shovel, which he had jammed into the sand. "Look, I'm excited to tell you something. I couldn't wait another second. It's thrilling, yet hard to accept at first. I won't blame you if you think I'm crazy. I found it hard to believe myself and thought that Kristoff was crazy."

"Who is Kristoff?" Bartels asked.

"I am." Kristoff looked amused, a friendly smile on his face. "But I go by Nic Kringle. Look," said Kristoff, "let's keep working so we don't draw attention to ourselves. We can talk and work at the same time."

The three men returned to their routine of shoveling, filling, and stacking the pile of sandbags, and Eckerd took the lead of the conversation. "Kringle here is not what you know him to be. First, his real name is Kristoff Christkindl."

Bartels instantly recognized the name, having helped Eckerd investigate his whereabouts months earlier. "Have you been drinking, Eckerd?" Bartels muttered. "So, you're saying that Kringle is actually your friend

Kristoff, that is dead?"

"Precisely," Eckerd replied.

"So, this Kringle is a ghost in front of me?"

"Don't be dense, Bartels. Clearly he's not a ghost."

"Well, if he's not a ghost, and he's dead, what is he then?" Bartels countered.

"He's obviously not dead and very alive. He has been using a fake name so he can be back into the war." Eckerd responded.

Eckerd drew in a long breath and held it in his lungs for a long pause before releasing it. "Look, Bartels, just hear me out. Try not to cross examine me. Just hear what I have to say, and then after you have the entire picture, you might understand a little bit better."

Bartels nodded his head in agreement.

Eckerd dumped another shovel of sand into the bag held by Bartels. After tying it closed, Kristoff tossed it over his shoulder and walked it a few paces away to the stack that was starting to build up. "Listen closely, Bartels. Kristoff was attacked by one of our own soldiers named Gunter. Gunter was always trying to get Kristoff in trouble and told his commanders and fellow soldiers that Kristoff was a Jewish-loving Nazi. Some of Gunter's cronies believed him. The truth was, Gunter was actually correct. Kristoff did love the Jews. In fact, Kristoff didn't hate anyone. He loved the world and the people in it, and hate was something I don't think he ever felt. I have seen him upset and angry at individuals, but it was usually aimed at someone that had been mistreating others. The way Kristoff sees it, we're all equal in this world. Brothers and sisters of a large family."

Kristoff returned to the others, grabbed another bag of sand, turned and walked away once again. Bartels watched him walk away, now feeling a little more curious about him.

"Keeping the story short, one afternoon Kristoff was sent on a special secret mission. Gunter had been assigned to follow him and observe but ultimately attacked Kristoff from behind, killing him and leaving his body behind. Gunter made up the famous story about how Kristoff was the mysterious Die Eule and how Gunter had outwitted and killed Kristoff."

Bartels stood and pointed at Kristoff. "So, you are the famous Die Eule?"

"Just keep listening, Bartels," Kristoff said, his back to him. "But, yes, I was, and I guess I still am."

"This is the part that is most interesting," Eckerd said with a grin and then proceeded to tell Bartels the details about Kristoff's experience in the hospital and meeting Santa Claus. Bartels stood looking at Eckerd stunned and slightly incredulous. At length Kristoff returned once again to the working men. However, he was holding a bucket filled with water and a metal cup. "Care to wet the whistle?"

Both men dropped the shovel and bag and approached Kristoff.

"Is every word true?" Bartels asked Kristoff.

Kristoff stared directly into Bartels's eyes as if staring into his soul and replied with a simple yes. With that one word, it was as if all the things that Bartels ever knew to be true in life had multiplied a millionfold and entered his body all at once.

Bartels's knees buckled underneath him. The next thing he knew, he found himself sitting on the sand slightly bewildered.

"I didn't think Santa was real," he muttered.

"We didn't believe either, but here we are. Bartels, Kringle is Kristoff, and Kristoff is Santa. He's real. It's all real, but not exactly as the stories we've heard. It's a lot to take in," Eckerd explained. "It was a lot for me to take in too."

"Imagine how I felt!" Kristoff said with a big grin.

All three men began to laugh.

"Wow! Santa is real!" Bartels said.

The three men labored for the rest of the day. Kristoff gave all the details of Santahood, forming a tight bond of trust with the two men. By the end of the afternoon, the men were surprised to see that they had filled several tons of sand into heavy bags.

"You know, the whole reason Eckerd and I are out here," Bartels said, "is to find Lorelei. Spy reports say she is close to here. Eckerd and I were going to sneak out at night, find her, and then the three of us were going to travel to Sweden. Tonight, we can leave and go get her. Why, with your abilities, and dare I say magic, this whole rescue mission just got a lot easier."

"She won't recognize me," said Kristoff. "The ring makes sure of that. I can't wait to be reunited with Lorelei. My heart yearns to be with her. But we cannot go out tonight," Kristoff said. "I'm going to a house to help out a Jewish family in trouble."

"Who are you going to help, Kristoff? I didn't see any Jewish families here," Eckerd said.

"I don't know where they are actually," Kristoff said. "I put on Guinevere earlier when I was stacking the sandbags. I saw this family hiding in a house somewhere. They were out of food and the children are terribly hungry. You might find this hard to believe, but my heart was so full of concern and love for this family that I found myself wishing with all my heart I could be there with them and help. A strange feeling appeared inside me. It felt like my navel was being pulled from the outside in. Things got really foggy, and my ears felt like they were plugging up. Suddenly I was standing in front of the house that I had seen a moment earlier. I snuck to the window and peeked in. I could see a young boy sitting on a wooden box next to the window. I removed my uniform shirt so I would not scare the lad, leaving my undershirt on. I tapped on the glass, and he cautiously peered out.

"I told him not to be scared and that I was Santa. The little boy smiled and let out a giggle. I asked if he was hungry, and he nodded his little head. I told him that I would be back with food tonight and to let everyone else in the neighborhood that is hiding and hungry put a small Scots pine sapling in the window as a sign, and to look for the man in the red coat to return with food. He darted away and that tugging feeling in my navel returned along with the fogginess and plugged-up ears. The next thing that happened, I was standing where I had stood before. I had time traveled and nobody noticed me leave. I think I understand time travel."

The last Maultier half-track truck clamored in the distance. The men turned and saw it belch out a dark diesel smoke. Kristoff checked his watch. "It's 15:35, gentlemen. Time to head back and meet our new commanding officer."

"Well done today," said Kristoff. "A most productive day indeed. Tonight, after supper, I'll grab my Santa bag and head back to that house to give food to that little boy and family."

"Santa bag? What is that?" asked Eckerd.

"A few nights ago, when I was dropped off to our platoon, it appeared in my gear bag. I didn't notice it right away. Not knowing where it came from or what it was, I took it out to inspect it. The fabric was softener than anything I remember touching before. The bag was red on the inside and black on the outside. It was reversible, I believe to help camouflage it. I imagine I could use it as a red bag in the future. The bag can extend as big in diameter and length as needed. When folded up it fits in the pocket of my jacket pocket. It is made of the most unusual material. I reached inside and pulled parchment out with an inscription. 'What you desire of want or need, can only appear after a righteous plea...'"

"What does that mean?" asked Eckerd.

"It means that I can only use it for good, not for self-serving purposes."

"Have you tried it out yet?" Bartels asked.

"I did. I reached in and asked for one of those American chocolate bars I have heard so much about."

What happened?" both men asked in unison.

"Nothing," replied Kristoff. "That is when I discovered it wasn't for self-serving purposes."

All joined in a heart-felt laugh.

The three men continued walking back to camp. The sun continued to drop out of the horizon.

"What about the red coat you're going to wear tonight, Kringle?"

"I've stitched the red portions of Nazi flags into the lining of my coat. When reversed, I have a red coat."

Both Eckerd and Bartels looked satisfied. "It looks like you have thought this through well enough," remarked Eckerd.

"I'm excited to finally do what I have been called to do. Come, let's hurry. It's almost 16:00 hours."

21

A Familiar Face

Eckerd, Kristoff, and Bartels stood patiently in line with the other soldiers of their platoon for their new commanding officer. The fatigued men were dirty and hungry, and every passing moment made their stomachs rumble. The camp was busy with men returning from duties, and the smells from the camp kitchen began to welcome in the evening.

The sounds of boots splattering in the mud behind the men grabbed their attention. Solidly in line, not one of the soldiers dared to look. From the sound of it, Lieutenant Heydrich was coming to introduce his relief of duty. The approaching men walked along the far side of the soldiers, and one of the men ordered, "Angetreten!"

Instantly all the men snapped to attention. The two officers made a sharp 90-degree turn at the front row of men and came to a halt at the direct center of the soldiers before giving one more sharp 90-degree turn to the right. Standing center and facing the soldiers, his marching was on point. Judging his exactness in marching, this commander wanted to impress his new men.

"Keep your eyes straight. No looking around!" the commander

ordered the men. "You are soldiers that follow orders, not a group of men here to be disorderly. You will give respect to me and the Führer we serve."

His uniform was an exact match of Lieutenant Heydrich's. However, the suit was well pressed, and his boots, though muddy, looked like he had spent the last few hours buffing them. "Lieutenant Heydrich has been dismissed from his duties. I am who you will look to for orders. Don't get comfortable with me, for I am here for a short period of time. I have it on good report that I will be transferred to Berlin to serve closely with the Führer himself."

It was all Kristoff could do to keep from rolling his eyes. *Man, this guy is full of himself.*

"My name is Lieutenant Müller and this is my assistant Unteroffizier Bauer. There will be respect or punishment of the most severe kind."

Kristoff's eyes darted to the left and rested on the Lieutenant's face, then at his assistant. A pit rolled around inside Kristoff's gut as he looked forward once again. Opening the right corner of his mouth slightly, he whispered to Eckerd, "It's Gunter and Hanz."

Eckerd glanced quickly at the officer and his assistant, and then gave a slight nod. Kristoff's fears were confirmed. It was Gunter and Hanz.

Gunter and Hanz began lecturing about obedience. They continued this routine, passing by each soldier standing in line, making smug comments along the way about the condition or looks of a soldier. Gunter and Hanz made their way toward Kristoff, Eckerd, and Bartels. Gunter stopped in front of Kristoff, his eyes staring at his snow-white hair that could be seen just below his cap and above his ears.

"Wie ist dein name?"

"Kringle. Mein name ist Kringle," Kristoff said, disguising his voice.

"Ha! Look here, Hanz! This soldier is Kringle, or Santa by the looks of things. Snow-white hair! Clearly, you're a freak of nature. Well, Kringle, you're the ugliest Santa I have ever seen. Just look at the scar on your face, dirty with sweat and sand. It's no wonder you have a scar on your face. Someone probably knifed you trying to escape your frightening face." Hanz laughed at every insult. The two men fed upon each other's cruelty.

"Yes, ugly indeed," Gunter continued, "but your eyes seem familiar to me. Have we met before? Nein, I could never forget that ugly face." With those last insulting words, Gunter and Hanz walked on to Eckerd.

"Look here, this must be ugly row. Why, look at those pointy ears and puny arms. No question, this was Kristoff's friend Eckerd. You must be broken up inside to know that he was a traitor. It brought me great joy killing Die Eule. He was obviously no match for me and my strength. Why you ever took him as a friend is beyond me. Do you cry at night in your bunk because you miss that old fool?"

Gunter and Hanz passed by Bartels and only gave him a look of disgust and snarky laugh. On and on, the two men continued until the last insult dribbled out of their mouths. "Not that you deserve it, but you are dismissed for supper. Lights out at 1900 hours. Dismissed!"

Eckerd, Bartels, and Kristoff walked together back towards the camp kitchen. "What is this all about? Of all the places Gunter could be sent in this war, he is sent here to look after us." Eckerd looked puzzled. "Something is definitely strange about it, and I think we need to look into this a little closer," said Kristoff.

"What's the plan?" Bartels asked.

"Well, it just so happens that being invisible has its merits. One of my favorite perks of the job. After I get back from delivering food tonight, I will sneak over to Gunter's tent and check things out."

The three men finished their dinner faster than ever before that evening. All were anxious to see magic in action and finally start something they had all wanted to do. Each in their own way had been helping Jews since the opposition began. Numerous lives and families had been saved by their efforts and thwarted attacks from the Nazis because they had been successful at warning the Jews in hiding. Investigations within their department searching for traders made things tricky and suspicions high. Eckerd and Bartels arranged for their own transfer and the beginning of an escape from the grasps of the Nazi army.

Leaving the dinner, the men rushed back to their tent. Bartels took watch at the door, and Kristoff grabbed his coat and Santa bag. Reaching into his pocket, he located Guinevere. Both Eckerd and Bartels now had their eyes glued on Kristoff.

"Okay, boys, here we go." Slipping the glasses on, red and green smoke appeared in the foggy glasses, just like in the hospital and on the beach.

"I want to go see the little hungry Jewish boy I saw yesterday," Kristoff said repeatedly. A small wooden-framed house of exact likeness from the previous day appeared, but nothing happened. No tug at the navel or foggy feeling. He wanted to go there but couldn't seem to transport himself.

"What's going on, mate?" Eckerd asked.

"Not working?" Bartels joined in.

Suddenly Kristoff remembered. The glasses would help find the needed time travel portal. He must have lucked out on the beach and had been standing in one when he put Guinevere on yesterday. Kristoff turned his head right and left scanning the tent. "There it is!" Kristoff said, walking toward the back corner of the tent. Both Bartels and Eckerd were afraid to blink and miss something. "I found the portal, and I'm stepping in."

His ears began to feel full and sounds around him felt muffled. His navel felt that unusual tugging once again, and instantly he was in front of the wooden structure he had seen moments before in his glasses. A small six-inch Scots pine sapling had been planted inside an old soup can and was placed just inside the corner of the front window. For onlookers, it looked like a simple garden experiment but to Kristoff it was the signal he was looking for. Kristoff turned his jacket inside out to reveal a red coat. Grabbing his Santa sack, he did the same and stretched it to his desired size. There for any to see stood a white-haired man in red, sporting a three foot bag over his shoulder.

Crouching low, Kristoff made his way to the same side window as before. Peering in, the room was dark but the flickering of a candle in a back room could be seen. Kristoff did not waste time. Tapping on the window, he waited for the boy to appear. The glowing candlelight slowly increased, filling the room with a warm glow. The little boy appeared but not alone. This time he returned but came with his sister. She looked to be slightly older than the boy and two inches taller. But their brown eyes and button noses confirmed the sibling relation.

The wooden-framed window roughly slid upward, sending dry flaking paint all over Kristoff. A small voice from inside the house asked, "Santa, is that really you?"

Kristoff said nothing, only smiled and winked his right eye. Reaching into his sack, he pleaded as the parchment instructed. "Please, I ask of you, feed this hungry family. Is there a fine goose within your contents?" The soft bag began to wiggle, startling Kristoff, and he retracted his hand. The sack made a few more jerks before resting silently once again.

Unsure what he would find, and hoping to pull out a fresh bird ready to cook, Kristoff reached into the sack cautiously. Each passing inch into the sack, he felt the temperature rise significantly. Kristoff could feel the edge of a metal platter with rolled edging and what felt to be elaborate metal work. The platter felt too heavy for one arm, so with some hesitation, he reached in with his left hand and grabbed onto the platter. With some effort, the platter came out, and on it was a fully dressed goose, hot to the touch, and ready to eat. To Kristoff's amazement and delight, he hoisted up the bird and handed it to the children through the window. Tiny footsteps dashed away and just as quick returned to the window. Reaching in the bag once more, he pleaded once again.

"This family is maybe large, and stomachs must be fed. Can you spare another morsel or even a loaf of bread?"

The red bag began to ripple and heave in a dance-like motion. The sides became tight and stretched to a comfortable size. Kristoff nodded his head in gratitude and thanked the sack for its generosity.

Reaching inside, Kristoff retrieved a soft loaf of bread, then pulled out a blackberry pie, jellies, fruits, and vegetables of all varieties. Rations of food continued to be provided until, at last, a small, flat, light-weight object was removed. Inspecting it closely, brown wavy vertical lines on top of a cream-colored wrapper outlined the label. Kristoff first noted the beautiful red letters spelling TROPICAL. Before he could think further about what he had picked up, dark brown letters just above and below the word TOPICAL read, "HERSHEY'S CHOCOLATE." Kristoff smiled as he read the label out loud, "HERSHEY'S TROPICAL CHOCOLATE. I did ask for an American chocolate bar, didn't I?"

Standing up, Kristoff placed the chocolate bar in the boy's hand and gave him one more wink. The little boy handed a folded piece of paper to Kristoff and returned the wink.

Unfolding the paper he read, "Danke Santa." That small thank-you written by a child filled his chest with warmth and moisture in his eyes. Kristoff grabbed his sack, tucked the note in his coat pocket, and humbly made his way to the road. A house three doors down had a small Scots pine branch propped up inside its window.

"Could this be?" he asked. Knocking on the window confirmed his suspicion. Just as before, a child approached the window. This time a boy about eleven years old showed up with giant blue eyes that appeared to be smiling. Kristoff felt more comfortable this time and his routine was flawless. House after house, he continued until sixteen houses had been visited and no other houses in the area remained.

Feeling satisfied, he removed his coat, folded away his Santa sack, and put Guinevere back on. Green and red swirling smoke in the lenses showed him a time traveling portal three paces away. An image of his military tent was in the background. Stepping in the portal, the tug in his navel pulled him back to his tent and placed him back in front of Eckerd and Bartels, who were still standing where he left them, staring intently at him.

"So, you going to leave or what, Kringle?" Bartels asked, sounding impatient.

"I have already been and now I'm back," replied Kristoff.

"Ah, come on. You're pulling one over on us. We never took an eye off you, never blinked. You never moved anywhere!"

Kristoff reached into the pocket of his jacket and pulled out the small, folded paper. Handing it to Bartels, he smirked as Bartels read the child's handwriting thanking Santa. It was all it took to convince his friends.

22

More Than Invisible

Kristoff sat on his bed explaining the event in its entirety. Both men fired question after question at Kristoff. Amazed and entertained, the men couldn't be pulled away. Before long, however, fellow soldiers began returning for the night, and the three had to call the conversation to a close.

"Well, we'll need to continue this conversation tomorrow, gentleman. We'll talk in the morning."

Kristoff gave the men a good night, made his way back to his bed, and lay down. Yet, the story kept playing itself over and over in his head, casting away any sleep. *As soon as the men are asleep, I'll head over to Gunter's tent and see if I can find out why he and Hanz are here.*

Kristoff reflected on Mr. Hayes and how he was invisible to others when he showed up in the hospital wing. *The power to do this comes from the ring,* he reminded himself. *I need to believe.*

Kristoff had tried becoming invisible three times prior. The first time he did it, his entire body disappeared except his legs. This wouldn't have been so bad if he hadn't been leaving on a transport vehicle from the hospital. The only person that noticed was the soldier across the aisle from Kristoff. The man screamed, swore that Kristoff was invisible for a few seconds, all but his legs, and tried to convince the others. It wasn't long until the transport vehicle turned around and dropped off the man for further medical attention. Kristoff felt bad but figured a little more time in the hospital would keep a Nazi from killing others. His two other attempts were done in private and slightly more successful. His entire body was invisible; however, a light ghostly appearance was all he could achieve. Tonight, had to be different. He needed to find out why Gunter was here, and he couldn't take a chance on being discovered.

In a way to kill time while he waited for his tentmates to fall asleep, Kristoff lay in bed, holding his hand above his face staring at the ring. He studied the jewels and admired the beauty of it. Soon Kristoff found himself spinning the ring on his finger and concentrating on becoming invisible. He thought it would be good to practice before attempting to enter Hanz's and Gunter's tent. As Kristoff continued to spin the ring clockwise on his finger, his body became more and more invisible. He stopped spinning and his body began to reappear gradually. Kristoff stopped spinning the ring and this time only focused on becoming invisible, but the results were less than successful.

I wonder, he thought, and started to spin the ring on his finger clockwise again while concentrating on becoming invisible. In no time at all, his entire body became completely invisible. *So that's it then. I need to concentrate and use my ring at the same time.* Kristoff lay in his bed satisfied with his discovery, but then wondered how to reverse it. Using his quick intellect, Kristoff began concentrating on becoming visible again, and this time spun the ring counterclockwise. Instantly his entire body reappeared. *Genius, this ring is, just genius.*

Heavy breathing and soft snores coming from the tent let Kristoff know that the time was at hand to snoop around. Concentrating and twisting his ring, he instantly vanished. Sitting up in his bed he walked past Eckerd and whispered, "I'm on my way to Gunter's tent."

Eckerd must have been in a deep sleep because he didn't respond. Opening the tent's door, Kristoff slipped through to the outside. Recognizing the officer's tent, he approached with caution. The tent was mostly silent, although he could hear a quiet conversation toward the farther side of the tent. It was too risky to enter, so Kristoff walked to where the sound was coming from and sat next to the tent wall to listen. Being invisible outside protected him from being discovered by patrols and security detail.

Kristoff recognized Hanz speaking, and he was certain this was the right place. Soon Gunter spoke, and Kristoff drew in closer to the wall. The conversation was nothing of interest. Mainly, Gunter boasted about how good he looked in front of the platoon earlier in the day, and Hanz agreed with his selfish compliments.

"You know, it won't be long until I will be promoted again, Hanz. Perhaps they will give me a personal chauffeur and car to parade around in. Things are looking good for us. Did you get a look at Eckerd today? What a joke that guy is. I can't believe we were sent here to catch him and Bartels. These two pathetic screwups couldn't do anything right. Perhaps intel got this one wrong, for once."

Kristoff felt his blood start to boil. He couldn't stand others being cruel or giving harsh criticism. Eckerd and Bartels were great men and extremely intelligent. Gunter loved to put others down.

"Still," Gunter continued, "if this allows us to arrest them and eventually leads us to Lorelei, the disgusting girlfriend of Kristoff, it will be all worth it. She has been running around long enough, protecting and helping the Jews escape from execution. I heard that last week alone she had helped seven large families escape the SS and provided them with documents to get to British-controlled Palestine. I can't wait to squeeze the breath and life out of that filthy Jew. By the week's end, I'll be able to tell headquarters that I eliminated Eckerd, Bartels, and that dirty Jew Lorelei. Down goes Die Eule and his followers."

Kristoff must have been listening so closely that he lost his balance and fell into the tent wall slightly. The conversation stopped, and he heard one of the men whisper that someone was outside the tent. He heard the men scramble to the door and were running toward his direction. Kristoff walked slowly away, knowing that he couldn't be seen. Gunter and Hanz inspected the area and searched around with flashlights. Once or twice, the beams from the flashlight went right through Kristoff as he continued making his way back to the tent.

After several minutes of looking around, the two men abandoned their search and headed back inside. Feeling it was now safe to enter his tent once again, he slipped through the door and lay back in his bed. His mind was racing from what he had heard.

They are on to us. They did not mention Kringle, but they are definitely on to Bartels and Eckerd. I'll inform them first thing in the morning. As Kristoff lay his head down, he felt a rumble under his bed near his feet. His Santa sack had fallen out of his equipment bag and was wiggling its way toward him. Kristoff reached down to retrieve it, and a small piece of parchment fell out of it. Grabbing the paper, he strained to read the words written on it in the dark.

Hungry families await. 18 houses adorned with Scots pine.

Kristoff sat up, reached under his bed, and grabbed his coat. Spinning his ring, he disappeared into the night.

Several hours passed before the sun began to rise. Eckerd and Bartels were sound asleep when the tent door flung open and Hanz entered.

"Get up and get going. Grab something to eat and be outside for orders. You have thirty minutes. So, if you want to eat, you better get a move on!"

Turning to leave, Hanz noted an empty bed.

"Where is Kringle?" Hanz shouted.

"He is in the latrine, feeling under the weather this morning." Eckerd did not skip a beat.

"Well, when he returns, give him my orders." Hanz turned and exited the tent.

"Where do you figure Kringle is?" asked Bartels.

"Not certain. I slept like a log. Don't remember a thing from last night," Eckerd said, while rubbing his eyes.

The tent door opened again. This time Kristoff emerged.

"Kringle, where have you been?" asked Bartels.

"I was outside. Couldn't sleep anymore so I wanted to be the first to see the sun appear."

Bartels and Eckerd looked at each other like Kristoff had lost his mind.

"So, you slept well, did you?" asked Eckerd.

"Sure did. I fed many families last night, returned like I had never left, and after sleeping a few hours, I felt so energized I had to get up. I think this magic stuff must help replenish me and keeps me going. I can't wait to go out again."

"You went out again, last night?" Bartels wondered.

"Sure did. It was spectacular. I also was able to obtain information about Hanz and Gunter. Get dressed. I'll explain over breakfast. Hurry now. You heard Hanz. Only thirty minutes."

23

Pointe Du Hoc

During breakfast, Kristoff provided the watered-down version to Eckerd and Bartels about Gunter's plan to kill them with Lorelei.

"If I could get my hands on Gunter, I would give him a piece of me," Bartels raged.

"I was angry just as well, Bartels, when I heard them discussing your execution," Kristoff consoled. "It's clear to me now that the same intel that you received regarding Lorelei's whereabouts had been shared with Gunter and others."

"But Bartels and I destroyed the information as soon as we received it, and we communicated with Lorelei through our own encrypted messages," Eckerd said.

"I don't doubt that you did this, but remember, we're dealing with the Nazi regime. Codes can and will be cracked," Kristoff said.

"While we're discussing Lorelei, may I share something with you, Kristoff? I feel you need to know more about Lorelei and the day she learned about your death," Eckerd insisted. "Months prior to us arriving in Normandy, I had heard about your death and had made it

176

my priority to find Lorelei. Bartels and I spent endless hours in pursuit of her, following every lead that came through the intelligence office. Eventually our persistence paid off. She had been discovered taking refuge in a cottage outside of Wiesbaden, Germany. Her effort to help anyone trying to escape Germany's grips were admirable as well as highly successful. During her short time in Wiesbaden, she endured many bombings by the Royal Air Force. I and Bartels sent out three E.L.F. members to verify her location. Upon our arrival, we entered the house unannounced. Reports back to me revealed that she was surprised at her discovery by the Nazi soldiers that had found her, but she never showed fear. The three soldiers shared with her the reason that they were there, that they were part of a small organization, founded on the principles and desires that Kristoff and her shared. They had also shared with her the unfortunate news of Kristoff and how he had been killed. Lorelei shrank to the floor and refused to eat for several days. Our soldiers never left her side. It took some time for her to build up her strength and pull herself together, though there seemed to be a heavy aura of sadness that accompanied her from that time forward. Her love was deep for you, Kristoff." Eckerd spoke with a soothing voice.

Kristoff swiped at his nose with a folded-up handkerchief and half grinned. "Look, Lorelei is unbelievably strong," Eckerd continued. "She, in time, was back looking for ways to help others. I believe this helped comfort her in addition to distracting her from the sadness. The first thing she did upon recovery was helping our soldiers get out of Warsaw and away from the war. She destroyed their Nazi uniforms and supplied them with street clothes, failproof counterfeit documents, and travel arrangements. The last we heard; our three men were in Denmark making their way to Sweden. Before departure, they instructed Lorelei to relocate to Picauville in north-west France, some 450 miles away. Bartels and I would rendezvous with her at the church of Saint Candide the last day of November at 22:00 hours, just two days from now. From there we have arranged for us to go underground where we have created an elaborate escape to the United Kingdom and eventually to Norway. Our hopes are to be united with Lorelei's parents. The last Intel we received before we departed Berlin placed Lorelei about twenty-five miles outside of Picauville. I'm most confident she will make it."

"Wait, if what Kristoff says is true about Gunter and Hanz, they must know that she is going to meet us there. In fact, they know the day and time we're meeting! We're all heading to a trap that we created," Bartels blustered.

"Outside everyone, on the double!" Hanz commanded the platoon as he opened the door to the dining tent.

Soldiers scattered in all directions in an attempt to get outside. Kristoff, Eckerd, and Bartels departed the tent and lined up with the soldiers outside.

"We were talking so much I didn't get a chance to eat," Bartels said, rubbing his stomach.

"I think you'll survive," Eckerd said with a cheesy grin.

The soldiers were called to attention the moment Gunter arrived. "It seems to me that most of you did not complete all of your tasks yesterday," criticized Gunter. "You'll return to your duties as before and complete them, or you can forget about eating this evening. However, one group did complete their tasks and will be assigned new orders." Gunter stood with his feet spread wide and arms crossed. "Kringle, Bartels, and Fichtmann somehow managed to set a sandbag filling record. You trio are now needed to help with stringing wire. Head towards the cliffs of Pointe Du Hoc. There you will find your orders. Don't keep them waiting. Dismissed."

The men departed and made their way towards Pointe Du Hoc. Arriving at the cliff top, a temporary site had been set up for metalworking, and various supplies had been staged in organized stacks. A man appeared with a buzz cut. He had dark goggles on his forehead and a leather welding apron around his waist. His dirty face outlined the goggle marks that had been pressed around his eyes leaving his orbits white and clean.

"Name is Oldenburg," he said. "Any of you have experience stringing Dannert draht?"

Bartels raised his hand. "Spent three months stringing that razor wire outside of Berlin," he declared, puffing out his chest with some pride.

"That will do just fine. I need you men to string razor wire at the cliff's edges to protect the hill tops from any potential enemy advancements from the beach. All your necessary tools will be located under those tarps next to that pile of scrap metal and pipes. The Dannert wire you will be stretching has already been dropped off at the cliff tops. You are grown men, you can manage on your own, just make sure you get back to your camp as instructed." The dirty-faced man turned and walked away, leaving Kristoff, Bartels, and Eckerd to govern themselves in their duties.

Bartels walked over to the tarped area with the others, peeling back the canvas that covered a wooden military crate full of tools of various sorts. Bartels began removing leather gloves, hammers, and a pile of staples for all three of them.

"The wire needs to be stretched along its axis to about fifteen meters. Three staples will be used to secure the wire to the ground using a hammer. This can go quickly if we work together. Let's put the staples in a bucket and bring them with us," Bartels instructed.

The men collected their necessary items and made their way to the top of the cliff face and surrounding ledges. Every fifteen meters or so, a coil of Dannert wire had been dropped and awaited for soldiers to be stretched out and secured.

"At times I wish that I could help the advancing forces obtain their objectives. It feels wrong to set up protection for an army I cannot agree with," Eckerd said.

Kristoff smiled tightly and began tapping his lips with the tip of his index finger.

"What's on your mind, Kristoff?" Bartels asked.

"I think we can help in our own way," Kristoff replied. "Why not try to help? We are setting up defenses, correct? Why can't we ensure that the wire is not unbreachable?"

Bartels flashed a look in Eckerd's direction. "That's it! We can ensure that a few securing staples are not so secure. I cannot guarantee that it will work, but it may just be enough to help at the right time. Let's see to it, gentlemen! Do your best to make it look secure, but weak enough to allow a breach."

The three men continued the entire day, extending the Dannert wire and carefully leaving just enough wiggle in the staple in a few areas to allow it to give way under pressure. At the most obvious areas, the men ensured a secure hold so as to not draw attention. Section after section, the men worked feverishly to complete their tasks but stopped to take water breaks frequently. While the men guzzled down water, they would take a few minutes to discuss plans for alerting Lorelei about the impending trap.

"I've been thinking about how best to let Lorelei know about the trap." Kristoff wiped the dribbling water off his chin and continued, "I think I can go tonight using Guinevere to find her."

"Do you think this is the best way to do it, Kristoff?" Eckerd swallowed his water down. "Think about it. She has believed you to be deceased and then suddenly you appear in front of her. You'll give the poor gal a coronary with your frightful appearance. It needs to be more subtle. Perhaps a letter or something." Eckerd handed the water cup to Bartels, who dipped it into a large bucket of water and gulped down its contents.

Kristoff nodded his head in agreement. "You're probably right, Eckerd. I didn't think about this. Perhaps, and even better yet, let's have you scribe a letter to her and sing it. I can leave the note next to her while she is sleeping. I can be invisible so she would never see me anyways. We can tell her that you, Eckerd, slipped in at night and left the letter but didn't want to wake or alarm her and possibly give her hiding place away."

"You think she'll believe it?" Bartels interrupted.

"Well, I don't think she'll have much choice, honestly. The letter from Eckerd, not waking her up. It's going to convince her. If the letter was from someone else, they would have arrested her on the spot after discovering her. I know my Lorelei. She'll believe."

"Why don't we just tell her where we can meet a day earlier and then we can avoid this whole mess?" Eckerd asked.

"I thought the same thing at first," Kristoff replied. "But since then, I have been planning something a little more favorable for us."

"You mean to say you have something up your sleeve," Bartels interjected.

"Yes, most certainly. As I see it, a plan was set to capture us, but what if we use this golden opportunity to counter their attack, setting our own trap in the process. We could be rid of Gunter and Hanz once and for all?"

Both men looked at Kristoff with great interest. "Go on. We're all ears."

Kristoff swigged down another cup of water and spent the next few minutes explaining his plan. Bartels took the cup from Kristoff and dipped it in the water bucket.

"This might just work, you know, Kristoff." Eckerd grabbed the cup from Bartels and drank it down, chasing away his thirst. "I agree with Bartels. I think this may actually be the perfect way to end our problems with Gunter. You can count me in."

Bartels snatched the water cup from Eckerd. "I was going to drink that, thank you very much." Dipping the metal cup in the water once again, Bartels joined in the resolute. "Count me in as well. Heck, you might as well call us the merry gentleman. We are on your side, Kristoff."

All three men joined in a smile of agreement. "So, it is then. Let's get to it this evening. Eckerd, you write the letter, I'll grab a few things I want to take with me. Let's meet out at the latrine around 21:00 hours. We must be as careful as possible. We cannot afford to draw attention. Bartels, you'll be on the lookout. If anyone heads toward the latrine, a loud cough will be enough to alert us of anyone approaching. Make it believable."

The three merry men, as they now called themselves, headed back to the Dannert wire to complete the day's tasks. Each one was now rejuvenated with energy in anticipation of setting their plan in motion in just a few short hours.

24

Gunter's Treasure

Lorelei had made the difficult task of traveling the entire way to Picauville. Once in town she was able to *find a secure hideout in the loft of a barn. The loft's* neglect was divulged in its lack of fresh hay, and the open roof exposing the stars and winter air. Lorelei had done her best over the past five days since her arrival in making small repairs to block the direct wind. The haystack was old and smelled of mildew, and smoldering dust would puff upward when moved. Lorelei had become very proficient in make-shift shelters, and this loft was no exception. With the help of discarded barn wood, she stacked the boards together like a childish tree fort, but it was only three feet high with its only opening to the near wall. With the aged hay, she covered the entire structure, which provided her with excellent camouflage and insulation from the elements.

The cramped area provided her just enough space to sit cross-legged with a slightly bent neck. It wasn't ideal; however, it gave her some sense of safety. Using her pack as a makeshift door, she closed off the night and switched on her flashlight. Lorelei had developed a nightly routine of looking at pictures of Kristoff that had been crammed into her locket. Removing her necklace, she pried open the heart-shaped container that held her most precious jewel. The black and white photo captured the angelic smile of the young man she had loved her entire life.

"Kristoff, why did you leave me? Why did this happen to us? Our lives and adventures were just starting for us. Now here I am hiding under hay in a barn for animals. I'll never forget you. I'll never love another. You have left me, but a part of me still holds hope that this is just a terrible dream, and I'll wake up in your arms, never again remembering this nightmare." Lorelei curled up on her wool blanket and switched off the dull yellow light. "Good night, Kristoff, wherever you are, heaven or near." The exhaustion of her overwhelming journey proved too much. Her lids pressed firmly together, and in an instant, she was fast asleep.

Miles away, Eckerd, Bartels, and Kristoff were lying in more comfortable circumstances but wide awake, rehearsing the plan over and over in their heads. Kristoff could hear Eckerd trembling in his bed just a few feet away. Kristoff was not the only one anxious and uncomfortable. The time finally arrived, and Eckerd got out of his bed, put on his boots and overcoat, and headed out of the tent. Kristoff listened as his footsteps faded the further he walked away. Kristoff began counting the three minutes down in his head. Each second felt like a minute to him. He knew in a few moments he would be seeing Lorelei and was uncertain how that would feel. His stomach kept folding into knots with each passing minute.

Time's up, he thought. Kristoff grabbed his coat and walked outside toward the latrine. The camp was dark and cold. Some small lights could be seen in the officer's tents—no doubt they were gambling. A set of latrines could be seen about thirty yards away, and a small flickering light could be seen inside the latrine on the right. The cold dirt under his boots hardened with the dropping temperature, making each passing step unusually loud. Kristoff approached the latrine door with a flickering light and gave it a knock. "Give a merry gentleman a chance at the latrine, will ya?"

Eckerd recognized the password and unlocked the door "The note for Lorelei is under the rock just inside as well as some rations," Eckerd said. "I snatched them from the kitchen earlier."

Kristoff nodded, entered the latrine, and latched the door behind him. A distant, though deliberate cough came from the direction of the camp that sent Eckerd's stomach tumbling. "Someone is coming, Kristoff. I can't keep guard here for you at the latrine. I got to get going. You're on your own. Sorry, pal." Eckerd scurried away, hoping to avoid any interaction with someone. If he was caught out of bed by an officer, it would certainly be unpleasant and cause for severe discipline.

Eckerd had only made it thirty feet before he was commanded to stop. "Why are you out of your tent, soldat?" Eckerd stood paralyzed. "Running away, trying to escape? Turn around and look at me!" Eckerd slowly rotated and found himself staring face to face with Gunter.

"Sir, dinner did not agree with a few of us, and I had to make a run for the latrine. Barely made it."

Gunter looked at him dubiously. "I have a hard time believing you, Eckerd. I think you're up to something, and I aim to prove it. When I am done with you and Bartels, you'll wish you were taken out a long time ago with your foolish friend Kristoff. Soon enough the German army will be rid of you."

Eckerd made a grunting noise, grabbed his belly, and bent over. "I think I'm going to be sick all over your boots, sir." Another grunt and cough came out.

"Get out of my sight, Eckerd. Don't let me catch you out again tonight."

Eckerd shuffled away, holding his stomach, out of sight.

Gunter entered the vacant latrine. Kristoff stood motionless, not knowing who was next to him. "Hanz, that's you in there, isn't it?

Thought I saw you go in. Just passed that goofy eared, Eckerd. He's up to something, I tell you. I think I scared him good. Should have seen his ghost-white face. What a joke that guy is." Gunter laughed inside the latrine next to Kristoff. "You okay in there, Hanz?"

Kristoff grunted in his best Hanz impression.

"Sounds like you're struggling in there, mate," Gunter continued.

Kristoff grunted again to acknowledge Gunter.

"You know, I lost tonight in gambling, but hey, it's only gold. After all, I've taken so much loot from being sent to the Führer during our raids, I am set for life. What's a few lost necklaces anyway? I almost won the whole pot tonight. I'll have to scratch that off my list of inventory so I keep an accurate account of my thieving." Gunter laughed again. "On second thought, I should probably destroy that record. If it accidentally fell into the wrong hands, it would not set well with the Führer."

Kristoff evaluated the situation. If he could step into a time travel portal, he could get back in time to run back to the tent before Gunter could leave the latrine. He had to act now. He quickly put on Guinevere, who gave a snarky remark of putting her in such a repulsive location. Kristoff began thinking of Lorelei and her location. Right away swirls of green and red vapor appeared in the lenses. A portal about five paces outside of his latrine materialized. Flinging the wooden door open, he dashed to the portal and was pulled out of sight.

Kristoff found himself standing inside a worn-out barn with beams of moonlight infiltrating the spaces between the boards. He removed Guinevere, folded her up, and placed her back in his pocket. A whispered thank you came from his pocket. Metal plows and implements had been abandoned on the far side of the barn. To his left, a rickety ladder was leaning against the upper hay loft. The barn was still and motionless and the evening breeze was sifting through the gaps in the wall. Kristoff twisted his ring and evaporated out of sight.

I know Lorelei is in this barn somewhere, but where? he thought. After searching the barn floor area and finding it empty, Kristoff carefully ascended the ladder to the upper hay loft. After ten minutes of looking, he began to believe his time travel portal must have made a mistake. Reaching into his pocket once again, he heard Guinevere complain about trying to sleep. Unfolding the spectacles, he rested them on his nose. Vapors did not show up this time. A transparent silhouette of a curled-up woman appeared under the haystack he was standing in front of.

Walking towards the wall of the barn and nearing the hay, he could see her pack blocking the entry. Putting his spectacles back in his pocket, it was all Kristoff could do not to storm inside and hold her close once again. His heart was burning and pounding inside his chest. He felt that any minute his heart was going to burst inside him. Just as he was about to abandon himself to his weakness and rush in, he heard soldiers talking outside the barn. He made his way to a larger space in the boards for a hopeful view of the men. A group of seven or eight men were sitting outside the barn resting. Several of the men were smoking and talking calmly. It was apparent they were not here to inspect things; they were only passing through. Their voices were muffled, and Kristoff could not make out what they were saying, though the men did appear to be wearing German uniforms.

Given the situation, Kristoff knew he couldn't enter to see Lorelei. He had to ensure she didn't get discovered. Kristoff quietly made his way back to Lorelei's pack and removed the handwritten letter from Eckerd from his pocket. unfolding it he read:

Lorelei,

Continue with your objective and arrival time. We have been observing you from afar. The enemy has learned of our dealings and plans to ambush us at our rendezvous point. A plan to ensure all of our safety and security has been arranged. Be on your best alert, but you must arrive at the time previously planned. I promise this will be one of the happiest days of your life.

-E.L.F.

Kristoff closed the letter and tucked it in her pack. Kristoff then laid the rations sent from Eckerd in front of the door. How Kristoff hurt inside. He wished he could let her know that he was alive and would be waiting for her at the church. Kristoff was about to crawl away when he suddenly realized he had placed something for Lorelei in his pocket. Reaching in, he pulled Lorelei's braided hair from his pocket and laid it on top of the bag of rations. "I think this might do the trick," he said quietly.

Kristoff made it down to the barn floor unheard and placed Guinevere on once again.

"Three times in one night. What gives?" the glasses complained.

Kristoff made his way to the nearby portal and instantly back to the outside of the latrine.

"You're all done already, Hanz? Heading back?"

Kristoff gave another grunt and then sprinted to his tent.

Bartels and Eckerd were in their beds pretending to be sleeping. Kristoff removed his coat and boots.

"All go well?" asked Eckerd.

"All is well," Kristoff replied. But all was not well. Kristoff felt heavy and lonely inside. He now wanted more than ever to be back with Lorelei. Kristoff got close to Eckerd's bed and whispered, "We're getting out of here. This plan will work. We need to get you, Bartels, and Lorelei away from the war."

Kristoff lay thinking of the strange conversation he had with Gunter and about his treasure he had been accumulating. He remembered Hanz telling him about his detailed list of items. *If I could only get that list from him, it would prove his guilt to the Nazi army.*

Kristoff abruptly sat up and reached under his bed for his coat. Opening one of the pockets, he took out his folded Santa bag and pleaded with it to provide him with the list Gunter had described earlier in the night. Reaching in his hand, he pulled a small piece of parchment paper. It read, "You didn't say please."

"You're correct, ol' wise bag. Please will you provide me with the list Gunter spoke of this evening?"

Kristoff lowered his hand into the bag once more. He didn't pull back a piece of paper as he suspected. Rather he pulled out a rolled up, bound notebook held together by a rubber band.

"Thank you," he respectfully said.

Kristoff opened the notebook to find page after page of a highly detailed list of items recovered from various locations, safes, and high-ranking officers. For once Kristoff could agree with Gunter. He was foolish to make this notebook.

Kristoff took his Santa bag, placed the notebook back inside, and asked, "Will you please keep this safe for me?"

A small paper shot out of the bag and floated like a leaf onto Kristoff's bed. Holding it up, Kristoff read the simple words, "Most certainly."

Kristoff thanked the bag once again and placed it back into the pocket of his jacket, then under his bed. Laying his head down in satisfaction, Kristoff drifted off to sleep.

25

Back to Berlin

Thе day had finally arrived for the rendezvous at the church of Saint Candide. Kristoff had spent the previous day explaining to Eckerd and Bartels about what he heard Gunter discussing at the latrine. His comrades were not surprised to hear about Gunter thieving around. However, they were flabbergasted to learn of the immense loot he had been stockpiling over the past several years, as recorded in his notebook. It was a lucky break for Kristoff, for up until that point, he hadn't formed a counter plan.

The men had spent the entire day working at the beaches of Normandy strategically placing Czech hedgehogs as part of the Atlantic wall. The large metal cross barricades made it difficult to postulate anyone would attempt to land on the beach and penetrate the barriers. The day had been long and tiresome, but now as they returned to base, the excitement of carrying out their mission at the rendezvous vanquished their fatigue.

"Today wasn't so bad, was it, gentlemen?" asked Kristoff as the soldiers positioned themselves in formation.

"Not bad at all," echoed Bartels. "I'm curious what criticism Gunter has for us today." A neighboring soldier chuckled in an apparent agreement with Bartels.

Eckerd leaned in close and whispered, "He might be particularly foul today. After all, he plans on this being our last day."

"Angetreten!"

The command came from the front of the men. In unison, the men stood up straight with their feet together. Hanz, pacing in front of the soldiers, was the only one commanding this evening. "I would like to recognize that Lieutenant Müller is not with me this evening. In his absence he would like me to inform you that while you were away, a tent inspection took place. You will find your belongings not where they were when you left this morning." Hanz smirked and unbuttoned his overcoat. "Lieutenant Müller has had something stolen from him last night and he believes the thief or thieves are among you sad bunch of lowlifes. Your orders are to make the tents ready once again. There will be no dinner or showers tonight. Perhaps a bit of hunger and soiled bodies might jog your memories of anyone that may know or possibly seen anything unusual going on last night. If the perpetrators are not named by first light, you can forget about breakfast as well. Dismissed!"

Grumblings rolled through the group of men as the Hanz stormed away. Eckerd was still standing at attention, clinching his interlaced fingers.

"Do you think Gunter could have found the notebook, Kristoff?"

"Not a chance, Eckerd. It's well out of his reach. In fact, it's no longer in my possession. Even if I still had it, the notebook would be hidden by magic deep inside the Santa bag and only I can retrieve the bag."

"Thank goodness." Bartels breathed out a pent-up breath.

"Walk with me back to the tent and I will explain." Stalling for a few minutes, the other soldiers paced away toward their tent. Kristoff watched as the last man from the platoon was well beyond overhearing. "We should be out of earshot by now. Let's head back."

The men deliberately strolled a safe distance from the others allowing Kristoff time to talk. "The plan is well in motion, my dear loyal friends. It took that dense Gunter a day to notice his precious notebook was missing. I can't help but feel a little satisfaction knowing he is in a bit of a panic."

"Do you suppose they suspect us?" Bartels asked.

Kristoff ran his fingers through his hair. "It really doesn't matter at this point, does it? If he had proof, I guarantee we would be walking to our execution at this very moment." Kristoff patted Bartels on the back, causing a thin smile to appear. "Look guys, early this morning, before anyone was awake, I slipped away to Berlin."

"Bbb...Ber...Berlin?" Eckerd stuttered.

"Yes, Berlin. I made my way completely undetected to office of the Nazi financial authorities, thanks to my ring. From there, I placed the diligently prepared bookkeeping notebook on the administrator's desk. I, of course, took the liberty beforehand to ensure Gunter's name would be easy to find. I also placed an unsigned letter just inside the cover of the notebook, informing the reader that this notebook was being turned in as evidence after it had been accidently discovered in Gunter's possession. The letter further informed them that one of our own Nazi officers has been stealing art, gold, and treasure that was intended for Hitler. I included that the purpose of the letter was to alert the financial authorities so that they could catch Gunter in the act of selling some of the art at the church of Saint Candide. Of course, all the details were included in the letter so they will arrive at the church when Gunter plans to attack us. Just to be certain, I waited around in the office unseen to ensure the bait was taken. Once the administrator read the note and began to thumb through the notebook, he picked up his phone and made a fury of calls. I guarantee they will be waiting for Gunter to arrive."

"It sounds like all is falling together as hoped," Eckerd acknowledged.

"Things are looking that way," Bartels said. "Besides, it's obvious that Gunter is allowing us to escape camp tonight. If you noticed this morning, he assigned us to patrol tonight. He wants us to make a run for it so he can be the hero that terminates us in town."

"Hey, look over there," Eckerd said, pointing at two Kübelwagens on the roadside. "Looks like Gunter even provided us with a get-away car."

"I was wondering how we would be getting to town," Bartels said.

"It looks like he provided you with a get-away car and a car to follow you in as well." Kristoff snickered.

"Look at that mess, would you!" Kristoff and Bartels turned their attention to the tent. Bags, uniforms, mattresses, and belongings had been tossed outside along with all of the other soldiers' stuff that bunk with them. Men were sorting through the heaped-up pile, picking up their personal belongings and moving them back inside.

"It's easy to see that Gunter is in a bit of a panic." Bartels' grin widened. "C'mon, let's get this mess cleaned up. After all, we have patrol duty starting shortly."

It only took about thirty minutes to get their tent back in order. Many of the soldiers were chattering about how unfair this was and complained about their hunger. Kristoff reached into his Santa bag and pleaded with the bag for something to feed the hungry soldiers in his tent. The bag twisted about and sent a parchment out the top once again. Bread and jams to fill the belly. Kristoff reached in and grabbed two loaves of bread and a small glass jar of strawberry jam.

Kristoff walked over to a thin fellow they called Maus. "You hungry?" he asked.

A few men looked his way.

"I have a few loaves of bread and some jam my mother sent me. You boys eat it. It's been a long day and I've had a nibble already."

Several men rushed over to Kristoff to get a piece of bread.

"Here, Maus will hand it out. There is enough for everyone."

Handing the loaf to Maus, men inside the tent began thanking him and smiling. It was a warm feeling of delight, the same feeling he felt inside his chest when feeding the hungry Jews just a few days ago.

"Kringle, Bartels and I need to get going on patrol."

Kristoff walked over to his friends for a last-minute review of the plan. "You two get going to Picauville right away. Once on patrol, take one of those Kübelwagens that Gunter so graciously prepared for you. It's about a forty-five minute drive, given the conditions. I'm sure your journey will be uneventful. Gunter has likely planned it that way for you. I'll meet you at the rendezvous point at 22:00 hours."

"You'll not be coming with us in the car?" Eckerd questioned.

"I don't want to draw attention. I can use Guinevere and a portal to get there. When you arrive, locate Lorelei. The three of you are to meet me behind the church. Whatever you do, don't go inside. Let's not bring violence into a place of worship."

"What's the plan when Gunter arrives?" Bartels asked.

"He'll likely want to take us inside the church and out of sight. Once he confronts us, I'm hoping the arresting officers sent by the financial authorities will think that we're there to buy art from Gunter and arrest him and Hanz. In the confusion, we're to slip out of sight and hide in a nearby house."

The three men acknowledged their understanding of the plan and after a quick handshake, Bartels and Eckerd left with their rifles and out of sight. Kristoff seated himself on his bed one last time and listened to the men enjoying the bread and jam. A small rumble from outside the tent confirmed his friends had successfully started up the Kübelwagen and were on their way to Picauville. A few minutes later, the second Kübelwagen fired up. Kristoff stepped outside just in time to watch Gunter and Hanz drive away in pursuit of his friends.

26

The Reunion

The last few days for Lorelei had been filled with a sense of anxiety while waiting to reunite with her friends. The discovery of her braid sparked both curiosity and hope. She had come to completely believe the letter from Eckerd; however, the braided hair was a mystery for her.

Could Kristoff still be alive? she thought. Not wanting to be disappointed and hurt again, she pressed the hope of him returning to her deep down inside. She continued to convince herself that the only reason the hair was left behind was to convince her the letter was real. *Why would Kristoff not have contacted me sooner?* Lorelei continued to battle her own reasoning in her mind, which helped pass the time in the barn all alone, but it also heightened her anxiety.

The morning of November 30 finally arrived. Despite her excitement and anxiety, Lorelei felt it would be best to enter town at sunset when she had just enough sunlight to see, but heavy shadows to help hide if needed. Many brick buildings lined the streets and towered above her in various directions. The streets were lonely in the evening with occasional passers-by. Those in the city appeared to be in a hurry to get off the streets and indoors. Nazi soldiers had been known to patrol the areas and cause stress on the people of Picauville.

Lorelei rounded the street corner, and her eyes immediately fixed on a peaked steeple capped with a cross. Multiple arched stone windows and steep sloping rooftops bore testimony of centuries-old architecture.

"There it is," she deduced. Her pace quickened and her stomach filled with butterflies with every passing step. Just outside of the church, she noted shrubbery and various types of vegetation behind the stone edifice. *That will work perfectly.* Lorelei bolted to the backside of the church and ducked into a large shrubbery. Forcing some of the shrubbery away, she created space in a well camouflaged hideout giving her the advantage over anyone approaching.

The shadows of the evening blended into a blanket of darkness all around her. Only the canopy of stars provided her light in her secluded vegetation. With each passing minute, Lorelei swore she could actually see the limbs stretching and leaves developing as she waited for Eckerd's arrival. Her muted meditation was finally interrupted by the hum of a motor and squeaky suspension of a nearing vehicle.

Observing from afar, Lorelei could make out a large boxy four-door vehicle with curtained windows. The back door flung open, and six men dressed in tall black boots, buttoned-up coats, and soft caps piled out the car. The car sped away, and the men, wielding submachine guns, dashed toward a building across the street and out of sight. Lorelei began to crawl out of her concealed area, but something compelled her to stay. "Stick to the plan, 22:00 hours," a little voice told her. Dropping to her knees, she crawled back inside the shrubbery.

The next hour passed as slowly as the first, and Lorelei began to question the voice she had heard earlier in her head. The sputtering of a motor and yellow headlights in the distance made her stomach knot up. A tan Kübelwagen came to a halt just in front of the church. The driver and passenger stepped out, closing the door quietly behind them. Two Nazi soldiers carrying rifles sprinted toward the back of the church. Squatting down and leaning against the wall of the church, a dark silhouette whispered loudly, "Lorelei, we're here!"

Lorelei's stomach instantly scrambled inside her, and her throat choked with emotion. Slithering out of her holding place, Lorelei darted toward the church's back wall and directly into the open arms of Eckerd. Months of bottled-up distress flooded to the surface all at once. Lorelei buried her face deep into Eckerd's shoulder and began sobbing.

"Lorelei, you're safe. It's over. You're now on your way home."

Lorelei looked up. Her eyes were red, and her cheeks were moist with tears.

"My name is Dennis Bartels, ma'am. I'm here to protect you on your journey home."

Lorelei reached for Dennis's hand and placed her hand in his.

"Pleased to meet you, sir."

Bartels's cheeks flushed and a smile stretched from his ear to ear.

"We can't leave just yet," Eckerd said. "The plan is underway, and Kristoff was adamant that we stick to his plan."

Lorelei felt a tug at her heart. "Did you say Kristoff?"

"Uh … um, I guess I did."

"Eckerd, don't you dare play games with me. This heart can't take it."

Yellow headlights appeared in front of the church and were shining toward the back perimeter wall of the church. Two doors clicked shut, yet the motor was still running and the lights remained on.

"Sounds like Gunter arrived," Bartels said. "It's go time."

"Quick, Lorelei, there's no time to explain about Kristoff but, yes, he is alive."

Lorelei's hand gripped Eckerd's, and all three stood up, turned, and walked toward the dim yellow beams of light.

Two dark silhouettes stepped forward, one holding a pistol and the other pointing a submachine gun at them.

"Stop where you are!" one of the silhouettes commanded.

"Gunter, Hanz, glad you could make it!" said Eckerd.

"Stille! Not another word from you pathetic traitors! Drop your rifles and kick them away. Do it now!"

Eckerd and Bartels complied, lowering their weapons. They pushed them to the side and out of reach.

"I see you have that filthy little Jewish girl with you. You made hunting her down and all of your executions that much easier. For that, I must thank you."

"Wait, what?" Lorelei gasped.

"Didn't your puny rescue team inform you of the dangers you would encounter if you tried to escape? I know of your feeble plan. We have been waiting for this day for such a long time. Now I can be rid of Die Ule's team of cronies and the Führer will reward me handsomely," said Gunter.

Bartels clenched his fists and tightened his smile. "You say you have known of our plan for a while, but I must inform you, we have known of your plan to ambush us. You have walked into your own trap, Gunter. Your pride and your overconfidence have led you to your bitter end. Tell me, Gunter, have you lost some sleep searching for your precious notebook?"

"Nonsense. This is pure Müll, garbage, pure rubbish, I tell you," Gunter recoiled. "Not another word! I demand silence."

Gunter stared beyond his three prisoners toward the back wall and squinted. Cocking his head to the side, he demanded someone to step forward. Eckerd, Bartels, and Lorelei looked back over their left shoulders and noticed a darkened figure emerging from the bushes where Lorelei had been hiding earlier.

The man stepped forward, allowing the headlights from Gunter's car to illuminate the white hair on his head and impressive red overcoat.

"Kringle, is that you? Don't tell me you were foolish enough to get involved with this despicable lot," Gunter murmured.

Eckerd stared directly at Gunter. Standing with his feet apart and arms crossed, he shouted to the approaching man, "About time you got here, Kristoff! I thought you would never make it."

Gunter immediately locked eyes with the approaching Kristoff and shuffled backwards a few paces. "It can't be," Gunter grumbled. "Impossible!"

"Kristoff, you're alive!" Lorelei shouted as she moved toward him. Lorelei only made it three steps when she heard Gunter shout, "Stop! Not another step or I will gun you all down!"

Lorelei stopped in her tracks, and Gunter racked his weapon, loading the magazine full of bullets.

"I shot Kristoff myself. I left him to rot in the woods. How could this possibly be the same corpse from the forest?" Gunter insisted, his face looking pale. Pointing his gun towards Eckerd, Bartels, and Lorelei, he demanded explanations.

"Some things just can't be explained, Gunter, and if they could, I wouldn't expect someone as dim as you to believe it," Eckerd said.

Heavy boots slapped the cobblestone behind Gunter and Hanz. The other soldiers stormed across the street. Demanding that Gunter and Hanz lay down their weapons, each soldier stood behind them with guns fixed on their targets. Hanz immediately tossed down his pistol and placed his hands on his head. Gunter slipped the gun strap off his neck and turned around to hand his machine gun to the arresting soldier.

Eckerd looked at Kristoff with a grin and a sense of redemption.

Suddenly Gunter jerked around and aimed his gun at the three unarmed victims. He pulled the trigger, spraying bullets in a small burst. Each body dropped lifelessly to the ground before another set of shots behind Gunter eliminated any further threat. Gunter fell to his knees and rolled to his side motionless.

Kristoff ran to Lorelei's side, trying his best to revive her. She lay in his arms limp and didn't move. Several soldiers grabbed Hanz and marched him toward their vehicle waiting out front. He knew he would be on his way to a military trial and an unknown future for his actions associated with Gunter. The moment Gunter fell to his death, the secret he had held against Hanz for so long died along with him. The secret that Hanz's father was half Jewish and had been keeping it hidden using a false name in fear that he and his family would be executed.

The arresting Nazi soldiers usherd Hanz towards their transport vehicle when one of the soldiers looked back at Kristoff, clutching Lorelei in his arms, rocking her. "Sorry about how this turned out," the soldier consoled. "I'll send someone to clean this up." The sympathetic soldier turned and walked away.

In the distance, Kristoff could hear a vehicle start up and drive away, leaving him alone in his grief.

Several minutes of silence passed before Kristoff could let go of Lorelei's body and check on his friends. Each one lay on the cold soil, pulseless and hauntingly still. In an instant, all he had come to love and protect had been taken from him. His heart cracked under the strain of such sorrow. Kristoff stood up and stepped backwards from his friends. Losing his footing, he fell back to the ground defeated. Kristoff felt something under him start to move. He wondered if he had fallen on an unsuspecting critter now trying to free itself from the crushing weight of Kristoff's body. Reaching under him, he pulled the wiggling varmint from beneath him. To his surprise it wasn't a furry critter but rather his Santa bag flailing about.

"Sorry, couldn't help my fall," Kristoff apologized. Suddenly a parchment puffed out of the top of the bag. Kristoff grabbed it out of the air and read it.

"A ring of immortality is yours if you seek, not just one, but a total of three."

Kristoff thrust his hand inside the bag and pleaded, "If it be so, and if it be right, please grant me the three rings, that I might preserve life."

Instantly Kristoff's hand filled with three rings bearing similar markings. However, they didn't have any stones. Promptly, Kristoff thanked the bag and began slipping the rings on his friends' right hand middle fingers, starting with Lorelei.

Kristoff stared into Lorelei's eyes, waiting for any sign of life. Breath entered her body once again and soon her eyes started to blink open.

"Kristoff, you're alive!"

Kristoff pulled Lorelei to his chest in a firm embrace. "Lorelei, you're alive as well!" Kristoff pressed his lips tenderly to hers and gave her a warm kiss that was well overdue.

"That bloody hurt!" Bartels grunted.

"It was more of a burning pain, I thought," Eckerd said, holding his bloody shirt at the abdomen that was now healed.

"How is this happening, Kristoff?" Lorelei asking, looking confused.

Kristoff winked his left eye at Lorelei. "We have a long journey to get to Sweden. There's so much to explain, and all will be explained along the way. Quickly, let's get a move on. We need to clean up and find new clothes. Others will be back shortly."

The four hurried down the street and disappeared down an alleyway of houses, leaving Gunter's body behind them in the dark of the night.

27

Dark Magic at Hand

"Did you ever make it back to Lorelei's parents? What about your mother? Was she with Lorelei's family?" Mr. Amesbury fired questions at Kristoff as quickly as an arrow leaving a bow.

"Well, after several weeks of travel by various means, we were finally reunited with Lorelei's family. Oh, you should have seen it, Mr. Amesbury. Her mother fell to the ground with weakened knees. Her father erupted in tears. As for my sweet mother, she approached me ever so slowly, ran her fingers through my white hair, and pulled me in close. I'll never forget her words to me: 'A mother never gives up hope.' This is something I have witnessed over and over again during my journey in mortality. Regardless of the mistakes, the hurt, or the loss, a mother never stops loving, stops caring, or hoping. A mother is full of divine love.

"My mother lived a few more years after the war before slipping away one night during her sleep. It was a tender time for all of us, but I knew she was reunited with my father, and I'm certain she was happy in his arms once again. You see, Mr. Amesbury, all must pass through death at some point. We can't escape this, not even me. Death is just a necessary step to take on the pathway of eternal life."

"Did you just leave the war behind you when you left the church that night?" James was jotting down the answers as fast as his shorthand could go.

"War against evil never ends, really. But to answer your question, no. I returned to Germany with a better understanding of my abilities and purpose. I did what I could to help break down Nazi defenses, camps, and rallied beside the forces to defeat Hitler. I wore many different uniforms and spoke several different languages. I couldn't change history, but I wanted to help shape the future.

"After the war's end, I reunited with Lorelei again. We were married and remained in Sweden for several years before returning to Germany in the mid-1950s. We always had enough financially to provide for our needs. The Santa bag always provided as needed or necessary. We purchased a beautiful plot of land in the mountains and there built a beautiful cottage for us as well as for Eckerd's and Bartels's families. Yes, those two had wonderful families as well."

"I noted it was Eckerd who brought me back to meet you. What of Bartels? Are they not all still immortal, including your wife?"

"You are referring to the rings placed on their hands. Yes, immortal they are until they surrender the ring back to me. There have been many more recruits along the way who have received rings, granting them extended life in such a noble and selfless way. This is how the magic of Santa continues. Many E.L.F.'s help worldwide by caring for the poor, and helping create miracles of all varieties. The ring only preserves life. It does not have any magical powers of the ring placed on Santa's hand. As for Eckerd, yes, he brought you back to this room and remains with me today, wishing to carry out his mission until Lorelei and I finish ours. Eckerd's wife and Lorelei have been best friends for many years, and she too wears a ring of immortality. Eckerd and his wife have three children who live in the United States, eight grandchildren and twenty-seven great grandchildren.

"Bartels was also kept alive because of the ring and helped for many decades carrying out the work of the E.L.F.'s. He had a beautiful large family. He had five kids and many of his grandchildren remain here in London raising families of their own. His wife helped alongside Dennis, providing meals for the hungry and toys to children on Christmas. She never wanted immortality and two years ago she passed from cancer. Soon after Bartels relinquished his ring, placing it back into the Santa bag. He was reunited with his wife once again."

"What about you, Kristoff? Did you and Lorelei have children of your own?"

Kristoff lowered his head lightly. "We were unable to have children of our own. We both have such love for children, and together, Mrs. Kringle and I love being Santa and Mrs. Claus. You may see us in the streets together, Christmas celebrations, and truth be told, we have even spent time in a mall a time or two greeting children and sharing in Christmas wishes. You'll always know it is us, because we are the ones that remind the children of the purpose of Christmas, remembering and celebrating the birth of our Lord and Savior. Have you ever wondered how sometimes an unexpected or unexplained gift appears? That is the miracle of Christmas, the giving of hope, the building of faith and believing in what can't always be seen.

"I have a question for you, Mr. Amesbury. Why do you go by Joseph Amesbury?"

Joseph was intrigued by his question. "What do you mean, Mr. Kringle?"

Kristoff raised only his right eyebrow. "Why don't you go by your given name?" Kristoff pressed him further.

Slightly astonished, Joseph said, "When I became a writer for the Gazette, I needed a pen name that looked good on printed page and would draw in mature readers. I took my mother's maiden name and my middle name as my first. Hence, Joseph Amesbury. I didn't feel that Nic Kringle could write about anything but Christmas, so I abandoned the name decades ago."

"I have been watching you for years, Joseph. Your great-great-great-grandfather and my great-grandfather were brothers. We share the Kringle family tree, and this is something honorable.

"Your Kringle blood as well as mine run through our vessels. Your attributes to the word have been remarkable, just unpublished. For example, I was there when you pulled numberless victims from the ash and fallen debris on September 11."

"I was on a journalism report in New York on that day and just happened to be there," Joseph replied.

"That was no coincidence, Joseph. You needed to be there. Don't you see? It's in your blood. You have always put others' needs before your own. Think back to all of your riveting stories published in the paper. How is it that one man can cover so many tragedies and just happened to be in the right place at the right time? It's not by chance, Joseph. There is more to the story here. I've been at the same locations helping render aid. To date, you've saved hundreds of lives in various ways spanning over several decades."

Joseph looked down at the floor, studying lines in the wood.

"I never counted how many lives. I always kept looking for one more save." Joseph's cheeks flushed and his lids filled until a tear breached, rolling down the side of his nose.

A gleaming white schnauzer interrupted the tender moment as sat on Kristoff's feet. "Ah, there you are, Louie." Kristoff reached down and rubbed behind Louie's ears.

"You named him Louie?"

Kristoff grinned. "I've always been fond of Louis Armstrong and his unmatchable trumpet." Kristoff beamed as he gave his dog another scratch behind the ear.

Joseph stood up rather quickly. "I best be going, Mr. Kringle. It's been a real pleasure meeting you and learning that we're distant relatives."

Kristoff scooted to the edge of his seat. "Before you depart, Joseph, may I ask one more thing of you?"

"Certainly, anything at all," Joseph said.

"Can you share with me from memory that accident that occurred on your way over here?"

"How did you know about the accident?"

Kristoff waved his hand. "Never mind that. Just share with me what you can remember."

"Well, I was walking down Piccadilly Street, chasing the amazing aroma of bangers and mash, when I looked down for a brief moment at some notes I had scribbled on a paper earlier that day regarding a story I was following. I must have been distracted because I walked right into the street and an oncoming bus nearly took me out. Lucky for me it only knocked me down."

Kristoff stroked his beard. "What more can you remember after you hit the ground?"

Joseph squinted his eyes. "Well, everything was dark at first and quiet. I must have blacked out. I heard muffled noises in the street that became clearer. I opened my eyes and saw this chubby old man extending his hand to help me up. Getting to my feet, a skinny fellow behind me said it was a miracle I survived getting hit by the bus. He thought I was a goner, I suppose. After that I made it to a cafe, ordered lunch, and a white Schnauzer appeared." Joseph looked down at Louie. "It was that Schnauzer. I would know him anywhere. Why didn't I recognize him before?"

"Joseph, sit down for a second. You remember the accident in great detail. Can you describe the old man to me that helped you get to your feet?"

Joseph sat back down. "Like I said, he was chubby and had brilliant white hair. He grabbed my hand, lifted me up, and was gone. I remember—" Joseph stopped mid- sentence. "It was you that helped me up, wasn't it?"

Kristoff locked eyes with Joseph. "Joseph, you didn't survive the accident. Look at your right hand."

An exquisitely beautiful gold ring with curious markings and gems appeared on Joseph's middle finger.

"The ring remained invisible until you were ready to understand and accept it. It's been there since the moment I placed it on your hand on Piccadilly Street. Joseph, you have been called of me, Kristoff, to take your rightful place as Santa."

At that moment, Eckerd, Eckerd's wife, Aada, and Lorelei entered the room. Kristoff reached into his pocket and pulled out his spectacles one last time. Handing them to Joseph, he replied, "Take good care of Guinevere. She'll be with you until the time comes for you to pass her to another. This is where we must depart, Joseph," Kristoff said. "I know you will receive strength beyond your own capacities and inspiration and intellect will help guide your way. Godspeed my friend." With those final words, Lorelei, Ada, Eckerd and Kristoff stepped out of the room leaving Joseph behind to process his new incumbent responsibility as Santa.

The room fell silent as the last foot exited and the door slowly clicked closed behind them. Joseph stared down at the new jewelry wrapped around his finger studying the intricate workmanship and jewels refracting light. Feeling overwhelmed from this information yet excited and honored, thoughts began flooding his mind like the Mississippi River emptying into the Gulf of Mexico. *Me, a Santa? How could this be? I don't know what to do. Where do I start? What about my job at the Gazette, what will I tell Ms. Dixon? Ms. Dixon, I should speak with her. She can be trusted. I need her help. But will Annabel actually believe me?*

Mr. Amesbury fetched his hat, stood and exited the same door Kristoff departed moments earlier. Turning back, Joseph took one last look at the magical Schlitten Gelato Shop that abruptly changed his life. To his astonishment there was not a Schlitten Gelato Shop to be seen. No sign hanging out front, no elaborate frosted window. A bricked wall with flaking paint was all that could be seen. *There never was a gelato shop,* he thought. *A magical shop indeed. It was all by magic. Oh, that clever Kristoff!*

Feeling peppy and enthusiastic like never before, Joseph darted past clusters of pedestrians filling the sidewalks, racing towards his office at the *Gazette*. Nothing in the world could distract him or slow him down, not even the smell of bangers and mash afloat in the air. Panting, but not exhausted, he eventually reached the door of his office and took a moment to catch his breath. What day is it? What time is it? Being with Kristoff in the Schlitten Gelato Shop, Joseph lost all sense of time, or even what day of the week it was.

Popping open the door, Joseph was rapid to observe that everything was exactly where he had left it. His piled-up papers on his desk were still overflowing, his chair pushed away from his desk, even his leather briefcase he had forgotten when he left in such a hurry sat undisturbed awaiting its owner's return. The most curious thing of all was that the clock was the same exact time, down to the minute, when Joseph last looked upon it when he had last departed the office.

"You haven't left yet," came the familiar voice of his trusty assistant Annabel from behind him. Whipping his head around, he stared blankly into her eyes.

"What do you mean?" Joseph enquired.

"Well, you're not going to make it on time to your interview if you don't get a move on," she replied.

"Interview?" he asked.

"Yes, you know, my note with directions and **(8:00 sharp!).** Why haven't you left yet?" she asked. Realizing more magic was at hand, he deduced that he was brought back to the same time when he originally left.

"About that, Ms. Dixson, plans have changed slightly. My question to you is, why are you back at work again?"

"Forgot my keys in my desk. It wasn't until I got home that I realized what I had done."

"I'm glad you came back actually. I have something I need to discuss with you. Do you have time for a visit?"

Annabel nodded her head in the affirmative and the two sat down at Joseph's desk. "I'm not exactly sure how to share this with you Annabel, so please hear me out before you draw any conclusions regarding my state of mind. Let me just first put this out there, no, I have not snapped or gone mad."

Annabel squinted her eyes and scooted forward in her chair. "Okay, let's hear it," she said.

The same incredulous look that Joseph wore when Kristoff made his solemn declaration now graced Ms. Dixon's face. "Before you say a word, Annabel, let me prove it." Looking down at his finger he twisted the ring saying, "Here goes nothing." Joseph remembered what Kristoff had told him about the ring and began concentrating on becoming invisible while twisting the ring clockwise.

"Where did you go?" Annabel blurted out, looking below the desk. "This isn't funny, Mr. Amesbury. What kind of trickery are you up to?" his secretary asked.

Joseph began twisting his ring the opposite direction and instantly reappeared in front of her. The results were exactly what he had hoped for. Kneeling down to the floor, Joseph gently tapped Ms. Dixon on the cheek to revive her. "Annabel, wake up, Annabel can you hear me?" Her eyes blinked wildly, her clammy hand reached out, and grabbed

Joseph's arm. "What just happened to me," she mumbled.

"You fainted when I vanished and reappeared," Joseph said. "Sorry for any alarm I caused you. I wanted to convince you and the idea to prove it to you just sorta popped into my head. Didn't really think it through."

Joseph helped his secretary back to her seat. "I need you to believe me, Annabel. As you can see, this was not an elaborate illusion. I disappeared by the magic in this ring," he said, pointing down at his finger. I know it's hard to believe what you just saw, but I'm willing to show you again and again until you are convinced," Joseph said.

"No, once is enough. I know what I saw, it's just . . . well, impossible, right?" Annabel said.

Joseph's eyes widened. "I thought the same thing, that is until I had my article interview earlier. Annabel, I have so much more to tell and show you. Please just don't pass out again. You gave my heart a good fright."

That evening set in motion a new working relationship between Joseph and Ms. Dixon. Mr. Amesbury resigned from the *Gazette,* taking his secretary with him. Using his savings, he purchased a charming cottage on several acres outside of the city and converted the house into a year-round Christmas tourist shop. What better way to hide from the public than in plain sight he figured. His earnings from his now popular shop provided the necessities of living as well as a comfortable salary for his one employee, Ms. Dixon.

During the six months since Joseph had been called of Kristoff, the duo had established their business, found innumerable ways to use magic to provide miracles, and help the less fortunate. During his first Christmas as Santa, Joseph jumped from history lock to history lock to provide for many adults and children helping ensure the spirit of Christmas was thriving. In each and every adventure, Joseph made sure to always give credit back to the divine origin of his gifts and the reason we celebrate Christmas. His motivation and joy was found in honoring and remembering the birth of our Savior. With the ongoing use of innumerable history locks, Christmas was not the only day of miracles. Every day for Joseph was filled with happiness and the satisfaction of service.

Today's events started out the same for Joseph spending the morning helping Ms. Dixon restock shelves with small Santa figurines and personalized tree ornaments. The small brass bell hanging above the souvenir shop suddenly rang out and a large figure stepped over the threshold of the front door. Looking up Joseph could barely believe his eyes. "Kristoff, is that you?"

Kristoff felt his pulse race as he stuffed his hands inside his pockets. "Joseph, be aware, Guinevere has shown me something most concerning, your possible successor. His face was concealed and not shown to me, so I know not who he is. Never before has the ring been removed by another mortal, and I fear dark magic is at hand, for I saw this marauder successfully remove the ring from your hand. The thing that is most worrisome is that I feel you may already know him." ......

28

ABOUT THE AUTHOR

Eric Johnson, a fifth-generation Arizona native, spent his youth in the Prescott area, often riding horses or casting lines in the local lakes. He pursued higher education at Arizona State University and A.T. Still University. Eric and his wife Barbara now live in north Phoenix with their five children, where they share a love for horseback riding and raising show steers for county fairs. Eric is renowned for his storytelling prowess, weaving intricate tales that captivate audiences with their vivid imagination and rich detail. Inspired by bedtime stories crafted for his children, Eric's passion for storytelling has led him to bring his narratives to life on the printed page.

www.ingramcontent.com/pod-product-compliance
Lightning Source LLC
Chambersburg PA
CBHW050322110726
47899CB00007B/2341